MW00627767

ON THE
ACCIDENTAL
wings
OF
DRAGONS

By: Julie Wetzel

I would like to dedicate this to my biggest fan. You will always be a bright light in my life.
I love you Grandma!

ON THE ACCIDENTAL WINGS OF DRAGONS
Copyright ©2015 Julie Wetzel
All rights reserved.

ISBN: 978-1-63422-457-4
Cover Design by: Marya Heidel
Typography by: Courtney Spencer

Chapter One

MICHAEL PEEKED UP AT THE NOISE COMING FROM THE door. It had been the first sign of life in this hellhole since he had been chained to the wall days ago. Maybe someone was coming to let him out. Or even just give him a drink. God, he was thirsty. It didn't help that he could see a small trickle of water sliding down from a grate to pool just a few feet away. Tucking away from his needs, he readied himself for some kind of action. He'd been through extensive training to deal with stuff like this. There were hundreds of things he could think of to help him escape; he just needed an opportunity.

The light from the hall cut a square across the darkness of the dungeon as the door swung open. Squinting against the burning glare, Michael watched as his captor threw something large inside. Without a word, they slammed the door and left. "Well, that went well," Michael scoffed to himself. At least now he would have something to look at as he died of dehydration in a damp cell. Why they hadn't just killed him outright was beyond him.

In the thin light from the small, grated window, Michael's eyes searched the bundle that had been left. Was it something he could use to escape? It looked to be a wad or roll of some kind of fabric. Pulling against his chains, he tried to get closer, but his captors hadn't left him very much wiggle room. In fact, they hadn't left him enough chain to even sit down. If he stretched himself out, the toe of his right boot just touched the edge of the fabric. He tried to scrape it closer, but whatever was wrapped up in the bundle was damned heavy.

He had started to succeed in pulling some of the fabric loose when the bundle shifted. Michael froze as hope slammed into his heart. Could it be? Was there someone inside that bundle? His eyes re-evaluated the mass. It could be the right size for a person, if they were small.

"Hey." Michael's voice cracked as he called to the bundle. He pulled against his chains harder and tried to poke it with his foot. Clearing his throat, he tried again. "Hey." This time the bundle definitely moved. Michael stood back against his wall and watched as the cloth shifted. A split opened up, and a pair of delicate hands slipped free. His heart soared as the material pulled back and a woman rolled out.

She was the most exquisite creature Michael had ever seen. It wasn't the dainty curls or the soft glow of her skin that made his breath catch, it was the possibilities she offered. His entire continued existence rested in her hopefully kind hands.

She let out a gasp of air and raised one of those delicate hands to her temple. Pain raced across her face as she curled onto her side, gasping.

"Are you all right?' Michael asked, pulling against his chains. Mentally, he kicked himself as soon as the words were out of his mouth. *Of course she was not all right.* He could see the pain racking her body as she wheezed. He wanted to rush to her and comfort her. If he could just get out of these damned manacles. Racking his brain, he tried to think of a way to help her. The men who had captured him had taken his jacket and guns, but had they emptied out his pockets? He shifted against the wall, searching, hoping it was still there. "Hey," he called to her again.

She lifted pain-filled eyes to him.

He shifted to show her the bulge on the side of his leg. "There's a medic kit in my pocket." It was only standard issue, but there was a dose of morphine in it.

The woman studied him for a moment before another wave of pain lanced through her. It took her a few minutes of deep breathing before she could

3

unroll again.

Michael's breath caught again as she pushed out of the material wrapping her. He had been right; she was the most exquisite creature he had ever seen, but this time, it wasn't her potential he noticed.

The gold and bronze of a sleeveless ball gown hugged her shapely frame as she forced herself part of the way up from the floor. Her porcelain skin was flush with pain, but even that didn't distract from her beauty. Unable to find her balance to stand, she crawled over and flopped down next to him. She pressed her back into the cold, stone wall and looked up at Michael. He could see the question in her eyes.

He nodded at his pocket. "There are painkillers in the kit."

She studied him again before reaching up and pulling the nylon pouch free. Rummaging through it, she found the pills and swallowed them down without the aid of water. After a few more deep breaths, she leaned her head over and rested it against the side of his leg.

God, she felt good. Her heat seeped through the canvas of Michael's pants, warming him. Tilting his head back against the wall, he closed his eyes and waited. The morphine would kick in soon to ease her pain, but she would probably pass out from it. That meant a few more hours until he could get that drink he so desperately needed. Rubbing his tongue on the roof of his mouth, he tried to work up some saliva to tide him over. He turned his mind to the woman resting against his leg.

Who was she? Overall, she was rather rumpled from her trip, but she was still amazing. Her golden hair was braided and wrapped up in an elegant twist on the back of her head. Little wisps of hair curled gently around her shapely face, softening her lines. She seemed oddly familiar, but he couldn't place her. *She must be someone famous. Maybe an actress or singer.* He shook the thought away. This group wouldn't grab someone like that. They were set on power plays and money. She was more likely the wife of a politician or the head of some state. That would explain the recognition. He'd probably seen her at one of the many events where his group served as security. He closed his eyes and tried to pull up her identity. If he just pushed, he could do it.

Movement from his side pulled Michael from his thoughts. The woman had shifted away from his leg towards the pool of water. His dry lips parted as she dipped her fingers into its silvery surface. He could just taste the water she had cupped in her hand. The tip of his tongue darted out to wet his lip as she raised her hand to her mouth and tentatively drew in that life-giving liquid. His heart sank as she spit it back out, coughing. God, there had to be something wrong with it. Michael let out a defeated sigh and hung his head. He would die hanging on a wall, just feet away from help. Maybe it just tasted bad. Hell, right now he didn't care if it was sewage, he desperately needed liquid.

The warm tingle of magic tickled across his skin, drawing his eyes back to the woman. Her fingers rested on the surface of the pool, drawing runes in the liquid. Michael's eyes widened. If she knew magic, they might have a chance. He watched in silence as she finished her spell before lifting another handful of water to her mouth. This one met with her approval. To Michael's surprise, the woman bent her face to the water and sucked up a great mouthful. Oh, how he would love to do that! He looked around for something she could use to bring him some. Maybe if she tore off a piece of the material she had been wrapped in, she could soak some up. That would just be heavenly.

The woman stood up from the pool and turned to Michael. Even though it had only been a short time since she'd taken the drugs, she looked a lot better. His eyes darted to the water. What was the best way to ask for the help he needed? To his surprise, the woman stepped close and looked into his eyes. Her amber eyes shone with compassion, and his mind relaxed. Somehow, he knew that she wouldn't let him die chained to that wall. His eyes fell to her perfect mouth. A bead of water clung to the corner, and the desire to lick it up overwhelmed him. Sure, those rosy lips, just slightly puckered, would make her mouth absolutely kissable, but it was the promise of moisture that made him lean forwards with the desperation of a dying man.

It was pure heaven when she placed her hands on his chest and rose up to meet him. The softness of her lips on his eased the cracked skin. Her wet tongue slid across his mouth, and he opened for her. A gush of warm water flowed into his mouth, and he clamped his lips to hers so not a drop could escape. Pure ecstasy washed through him with that first sip. Shuddering, Michael swallowed what she offered. Honeyed wine could never taste as good as her mouth and that water. Desire shot through him, and he could feel himself stiffen as she pulled away. The woman let out a little puff of air, like a silent laugh, as she turned away to get him more water.

Michael's eyes dropped to the front of his pants. How was it possible to get a hard-on when he was so dehydrated? He was still fully dressed in black cargo pants and a T-shirt, and they were, so far, still hiding his growing arousal. But that laugh made him think she knew what had passed through his mind.

7

His eyes traced the gentle curve of her backside as she bent to draw up more water. God, how he wanted out of those manacles! To be able to lift the folds of her skirt up, exposing more of that pale skin. To feel her warmth and wetness as he pushed into her. Michael shook his head hard, trying to dislodge the image that had settled into his brain. How could he be thinking of her like that? For God's sake, he had just met the woman. She was giving him water, not making out with him.

Michael nearly died when she pressed her mouth to his for that second drink. He pulled against his chains with the desire to hold her. To explore that wonderful mouth. Would her skin be as soft as her lips? Would she fit against him? Would the rest of her taste as good as her lips? He ached to find out. She pulled away, leaving him bereaved for her touch. Gasping for air, he hung from his chains. A note of concern filtered into his lust-laden thoughts. What the hell was he doing? This wasn't him. Sure, he fantasized about beautiful women, like any man, but it never went this far. When she came back with the third mouthful, he rounded up his scattered wits and pulled away from her.

"What are you doing to me?" He gasped.

Her eyes filled with a compassionate sorrow, and she made a sign with her hand. A sign that the entire world had learned almost two decades ago: *dragon*.

His mind clicked into gear. That explained everything. The magic, his hormonal response, and why this group would kidnap her. She was a dragon. Giving in to his uncontrollable urges, he pressed back to her lips to claim her gift. No human stood a chance against a dragon; the pheromones they put out could send even the Pope into a mating rut. Hell, the stuff was currently making the rounds as the latest designer date-rape drug. It was fast, effective, left no side effects, and was hard to prove in court. It was ironic that he would be caught in this potent chemical's clutches. He had been working to stop the organization producing it before being captured. He shivered again as she released his lips. This was going to make things hard, both literally and figuratively.

Normally, dragons didn't put out a significant amount of the chemicals to bother people casually, it had to be harvested and refined to be used as a drug, but a dragon could pass it on intimately with the same effects. He was probably getting a significant dose along with the water from her mouth. Had he known she was a dragon, he would never have let her feed him water that way. His boss was a dragon, and Michael had seen how uncontrollable women got after he kissed them. It was most definitely a good thing that his hands were chained above his head. Sure, he was going to have one hell of a case of blue balls, but at least she would be safe from him. The problem would come when they tried to escape.

Given several days and a few good hand jobs, he could work the pheromones out of his system, but did they have the time? Now that she was here, their captors would have to act. There was no way they could leave a dragon with magic in a cell. Even if they warded the area, it was only a matter of time until they got free. The problem would be him. When she did get him free of his cuffs, he would probably fall on her like a satyr among nymphs. He had seen it happen with others. It was not something he wanted to subject her to. She would probably understand, most dragons under those circumstances did, but he would hate himself for it.

Anguish rode Michael right along with the lust as she pressed into him with another mouthful of water. He needed this—without the water, his death was almost certain—but knowing that his response was chemically induced didn't ease the guilt plucking at him.

This mouthful slid bitterly across his tongue as he worshiped at her lips. The liquid burned his throat, leaving him gasping as she pulled away. Something was definitely different about that sip. He tracked the heat as it slid down and bottomed out in his stomach. She reached up and touched his cheek, pulling his gaze to her. Shock filled him as their eyes met. Apology shone clearly in her face as his stomach clenched in pain. Groaning, he tried to curl up as his insides began to boil. He barely noticed when she leaned into him, pressing his back to the wall and taking his weight from the manacles. God, what had she done to him?

Now she'd done it. Carissa pushed up against the unconscious man. She should have gotten him down before she had worked her magic, but that would have led to a whole different bundle of problems, and they were all her fault. She hadn't thought when she drew up that first mouthful of water and passed it to him. She didn't deal with humans much on a personal level and had forgotten the effect dragons could have on them. It also didn't help that this one, with his dark, wavy hair and chocolate-brown eyes, hit every one of her yummy buttons.

She felt horrible as she held him up. All those sculptured muscles were loose under her hands. The only portion of him that wasn't limp pressed into her stomach where she leaned against him. Even unconscious, her pheromones made him hard. She ran her hand over the ridge in his pants. He was definitely a prime specimen of his species. Half considering helping him into a softer state, she shook her head and decided against it. He would probably be very upset with her when he woke up. Taking advantage of his helplessness would not help her case.

Pushing his body up, Carissa scratched a rune into his cuffs, weakening them. Working her fingers in next to his skin, she tore through the metal of the manacles pinning him to the wall. She shook her head as she lowered him to the floor. That should have been the first thing she had done. It would have solved a plethora of problems they now had to face. The disorientation and pain from whatever had been used to knock her out still tickled at the back of her head. The morphine from the man's medical pack had helped, but those drugs didn't work very well on her system.

Carissa arranged the man on his back and went to get another drink of water. The foul taste had started to return from where more water was dribbling in from the grate high in the wall. She would have to spell the water again when her companion woke up. He desperately needed it.

Putting her back against the cold wall, she pulled the man up so his head rested in her lap. Her eyes fell on the material on the floor. A curtain from the baron's house. She pulled the loose material over and wrapped part of it over her shoulders before spreading the rest over her companion. Tilting her head back, she tried to remember what had happened.

A ball. Carissa had gone to a ball held by Baron Estivis. That explained the excruciatingly tight corset squeezing her ribs. Why did everyone expect dragons to wear older fashions? Sure, the gowns were gorgeous, but they were so damned uncomfortable. Why couldn't she just have one of those nice cocktail dresses or an evening gown? Oh, but no, she was expected in a Victorian dress, complete with corset and impossibly long skirts. Shaking away her fashion worries, she closed her eyes and tried to remember what had happened at the ball.

Lots of dancing. Carissa had gone to the ball as a favor to her brother, Kyle. He had made other arrangements for that evening long before receiving the invitation, but Baron Estivis was a big supporter of dragons. This ball was a must for at least one of them. Since Kyle was busy, she had been given the duty. At least she had been saved from idle conversation. She couldn't speak without the help of her best friend, Tilly. The poor girl was down with a slight cold that prevented her from going to the ball. But, Carissa didn't recall anything sordid happening. It had been a pleasant evening filled with good food, wine, and lots of dancing.

Carissa ran her hand under the material to the small pattern embroidered on the man's black shirt. She had noticed the sidewise eight with a line running through the middle on the med kit. A smile curled her lips. Someone had really put some thought into the logo for the mercenary group that protected and policed dragons. It was simple, yet illustrated the group's name so well. Infinity over time—Eternity. They had really messed up this time—both with allowing her kidnapping and losing one of their own.

She looked down at the sleeping man. Goodness, he was handsome. She couldn't remember ever seeing him, but Eternity was known for staying in the background. In fact, most people didn't even know the group existed. She studied the scruff on his face. It had to be at least a few days old. Daniel, the head of Eternity, hadn't mentioned anything about losing a man when they'd last spoken, but that was more her brother's business then hers.

Brushing the unruly hair back from his forehead, she pondered over her mystery man. Did Daniel even know he was missing? Were they looking for him? Hopefully he wasn't too high up in Eternity. Carrisa bit her lip as a very bad thought hit her. *Pease don't let him be an Elite.* Daniel was going to be really pissed if she had just ruined one of his specially trained enforcers.

Slipping her hand down to rest on his chest, she leaned back and closed her eyes. Who he was didn't matter anymore. What was done was done. Daniel would just have to deal with the change in his rosters. And, if they were very lucky, her mystery man would adjust to his new life quickly. Now she just needed to rest for a while until he woke up.

Chapter Two

WHAT THE HELL HAD HE DONE LAST NIGHT? MICHAEL worked his sleep-addled brain, trying to clear it. A foul taste clung to the back of his tongue, and his head throbbed like he had been out with two hookers and a liter of vodka. Groaning, he rolled his head, trying to get comfortable. His pillow was soft and smelled wonderful, even if the bed was much too hard. He buried his face deep in the warmth and breathed it in. A soft touch brushed his hair back from his face. Apparently, the hookers were still around. He let out a sigh of pleasure and opened his eyes.

An expanse of gold and bronze material filled his vision. Rolling his head slightly, Michael looked up into the amber eyes of the dragon lady. Realization shot through his numb brain, and he cursed as he rolled out of her lap. Scooting back as far from her as he could get, he tucked his hands and face into a corner. Maybe if he didn't look at her, he could resist the desires she provoked in him. Why the hell had she let him loose? She was a dragon. She should know what kind of response to expect out of a human male.

Michael curled in on himself as he listened to the rustle of her skirt. The tingle of magic washed over his skin, making him want to peek at her. *God, what was she doing over there?* The rustling came closer, and he held on tightly, praying he could resist the lust he knew was about to slam into him. Any moment now, he was going to turn into a raging beast. Any moment. The hem of her skirt brushed his leg, and he clenched his teeth, waiting.

Cold droplets of water skated over his head and down his neck. The seconds ticked by as she dribbled more of the water over him. Unable to resist the urge any longer, he turned his face upwards, and she squeezed the rest of the water from the cloth into his mouth. God, that tasted good. Not nearly as good as it had coming out of her mouth, but it would definitely do.

The dragon lady reached her hand down and touched him. A tingle of desire rushed through him, but it wasn't the same, uncontrollable urge he had felt earlier. This he could handle. Grasping one of his hands, she urged him up with a silent touch.

Unfolding from the floor, he let her pull him over to the pool. The thought of water pushed all other desires from his mind, and he fell to it, drinking greedily.

Once he had had his fill of the water, he pulled out a great handful and scrubbed it into the skin of his face. Oh, it felt good to be somewhat clean again. A soft cloth rubbed against his hand. He took it up and dried his face on it. Opening up his now-dry eyes, he found the piece of cloth was one of the layers of underskirt on the dragon lady's dress. The real shocker came when he realized that she was still wearing it. He dropped the material as if it had burned him and backed away from her. Now that his need for water was taken care of, he could feel the need for her rising in him again.

"I'm sorry," Michael apologized. "I didn't know that was your skirt. I would never have touched it if I had." His mouth kicked into overdrive, and he prattled on about the water and the faux pas of using her skirt as a towel, trying to keep his mind off where it really wanted to go.

Amusement burned in her amber eyes, and she leaned forwards to touch his shoulder.

His words froze on his lips as she looked into his eyes. Letting out a deep sigh, Michael closed his eyes and scrubbed his hand through his hair. He shouldn't let her affect him like this. He was an Elite, damn it! He worked with dragons every day! Taking a deep breath, he centered himself before meeting her eyes again.

"Sorry about that," he apologized again, this time much more controlled. "It's been a long week." He smiled weakly at her, holding out his hand. "I'm Michael, by the way."

She gave him an understanding smile that stole his breath and shot heat straight to his groin. Taking his outstretched hand, she pulled him to his feet. Her hand felt so good in his, but he resisted the urge to pull her into his arms.

"Thank you." He let himself reach out and touch her shoulder in gratitude. "For everything."

Reaching up, she touched his cheek softly.

God, he wanted to roll his face into that warm touch, but he resisted the urge. Maybe her pheromones weren't affecting him as badly as he had thought. He just had to keep from kissing her again.

Sorrow filled her eyes, and she shook her head before turning away from him.

Confused, he followed as she led him to the door. "What's your name?" Michael asked as she leaned her head against the wood.

She shushed him softly so she could hear into the room beyond. Her fingers traced runes into the surface as she listened.

He shut up. The mystery of her identity could

wait until they were someplace safer. If she could get him out of this cell, he could get her out of whatever building they were in.

As soon as she had finished her design, the runes in the door flashed bright red. She stepped back into Michael as heat raced across the wood.

His hand went to her hip to steady her. Something down low throbbed, and he pulled her back against his body as the door turned to ash. God, she felt good against him. Okay, maybe her pheromones *were* working on him, but he could handle this. The urge to hold her was there, but it wasn't the same unbearable passion he had felt earlier.

Bouncing on the balls of her feet, his dragon lady flashed him a dazzling smile before grabbing his hand and pulling him to the door.

His training kicked in, overriding his desire. She was dragon, and he was Eternity. It was his job to protect her, no matter who she was. Stopping her short, Michael pulled her back against him before she could get through the door. "Let me go first." He turned so he was ahead of her and eased himself past the doorjamb. No one was in the outer room, but something caught his eye. Carefully, watching for enemies, he crossed the room to a pile of discarded items—his jacket and gear. The guns were missing, but there was a collection of other things in the pockets that could help. He pulled the empty shoulder holster on before slipping into his leather coat. God, he loved this coat. Turning back to his dragon lady, he considered the curve of her bare shoulders and the weight of the biker leathers he had just donned. He really should offer it to her, but that would make quick access to his tools harder. Weighing the options, he chose to keep the coat; she could have it once they were out of danger.

"Let's go." Michael took up her hand and led her out. Peeking around the corner, he pulled her around and down the empty corridor. They passed through two more stone halls without signs of life. He was starting to think their escape would be easy when a man turned the corner and practically ran into the pair.

Michael snatched the man's head and gave it a quick snap sideways before he could cry out a warning. He hadn't really thought about his actions or his dragon lady's response to it before he acted. As the body crumpled to the floor, Michael turned to take in her feelings. To his utmost surprise, she had already bent to the body to search it.

Pulling a gun and two clips from the man's body, she silently passed them up to Michael.

With a shake of his head, he took them. He should have known the death wouldn't affect her.

Most dragons, especially the old ones, lived by different morals. They were apex predators who didn't mind toying with their food before they ate. Hell, if she were old enough, she had probably eaten a few mortals along the way. He pushed that thought away.

Leaving the dead man in one of the side rooms, Michael and his dragon lady took off down the hall. A set of steps led up. The window in their cell had been set high in the wall, so they must be underground. Michael led the way up the steps and stopped just out of sight of the next room. This was going to be an issue. The steps opened up into some form of barracks. There were several voices. He tried to count. Maybe ten or fifteen. He checked the one weapon he had. There were definitely not enough bullets. Turning back, he pressed his dragon lady back down the steps. They would just have to find another way out.

His efforts met with resistance as she pushed forwards to look into the room. He hissed a warning to her and tried to pull her back down the steps.

Waving him away, she lowered herself to the steps and inched forwards to get a better idea of what they were dealing with.

He tugged at her skirt, trying to get her to come back. "We can't get out that way," Michael whispered, "come on." If they didn't get off these steps fast, someone was going to look over and see them. Then their goose was really going to be cooked. To his relief, his dragon lady inched back to his side. "We'll find another way out." He started back down the steps, but stopped when she grabbed his shoulder. He turned to urge her on and was shocked when her lips descended to his.

Uncontrollable desire shot through him, and he snaked his arms around her back, deepening the kiss. Oh man, she tasted as good as he remembered. His body thumped as she molded herself to him. Obviously, she was just as affected by him as he was by her. He explored the inside of her mouth for a moment longer before rational thinking slammed into his brain. They were kissing just steps from the same people who had tossed them both into a dungeon. Ripping his lips from hers, he held her close, trying to regain his control. Her heavy breathing didn't help, but the voices from behind her kept him from leaning back in to continue.

Finally, she sighed and nodded her head at him. She had regained control. *Good.* Dropping his arms, he disentangled them and went to step back. He definitely needed the space. Maybe he could quietly readjust himself as they went back down the steps. His pants had become uncomfortably tight. His dragon lady leaned towards him and snatched a quick kiss from his lips before turning back to stride purposefully up the steps, straight into the enemy-filled room.

Carissa heard Michael suck in a breath to stop her, but the warning he tried to shout went unsaid. He couldn't. She had his voice. She hadn't intended to let the kiss go that far, but oh, did it feel good. The touch of his hands on her back had tingled, like a well-placed spell. Her insides still quivered, but she pushed the thoughts and feelings back as she stepped from the stairway to the room. Michael was just inches behind her, and, if she didn't get out there now, he would pull her back, ruining her opportunity to act. She was sure he wouldn't let her try this if he knew what she was going to do.

The room fell silent as the men inside were startled by her sudden appearance. Carissa had just a moment to act before someone's brain clicked into gear and all hell broke loose. Opening her mouth, she let the first strands of ancient langue slip out. She wove her power into the song as it rose from her chest. There were very few that still understood the words she sang, but no human could escape its power. She walked to the middle of the room and stood, forcing the magic out.

At first, she had thought her kidnapping must have been an error. No one in their right mind would kidnap her. Her brother would be furious when he found out. But now she was sure she was the intended target. The spells she'd woven on the water and door should have been very simple, but she'd had to pull out high runic magic to accomplish the tasks. Someone had warded these people against lower forms of magic. It made things harder, but that wouldn't stop her. She had gone into this room expecting to find the same level of protection on air magic, but the spell slipped easily from her. Only someone that knew her weakness would leave such a vast field of magic open. You could do so much more with air magic, but you had to have a voice to use it.

Never underestimate your opponent. Whoever had kidnapped her had definitely underestimated her. Carissa turned part of her attention to the man standing, shocked, in the doorway. Michael. She was going to have a lot of explaining to do. If he hadn't realized who she was before, he surely did now. Maybe if she were lucky, he would save his questions until they were out of this mess. Or maybe she should just keep his voice for a while so he couldn't ask them.

Pressure in the air drew Carissa's attention back to her task. There was a mage somewhere in this

25

room, fighting back. She looked around at the passive faces. Turning a full circle as she sang, she looked for him. Whoever he was, he was strong. She poured her full strength into the strange words and pushed it back up the stream of power working against her. He let out a croak of pain as her power reached him and tore through his brain. That was one mage who wouldn't trouble her again. Now, she just had to finish subduing the rest of them and get out of here. The first of her kidnappers slumped to the floor, unconscious.

It was taking too much raw power to put these men down. Carissa looked around as the last of them crumpled to the floor. Normally, she would just kill them all with a few words and be done with it, but whatever they had used to subdue her in the first place was still working on her system. It had only been a few hours since she'd pushed out of that curtain cocoon. Maybe she should have waited until tomorrow to try escaping. *Too late now.* She pushed the rest of her power out to make sure none of the men woke up as they took their leave.

Swaying on her feet, Carissa crumpled to the floor, too. She just needed a few minutes in a lower state to recover. The transformation should help her, but it was going to make Michael's job harder. Hopefully, he was up to the challenge. She closed her eyes to let go of part of her control.

Chapter Three

OH GOD! OH GOD! OH GOD! MICHAEL'S BRAIN chanted as his dragon lady stepped into the room filled with enemies. The first strands of sound hit him, and he knew. God, he knew who she was! How had he not recognized her? *Who in their right mind would kidnap her?* And he had kissed her! Oh God, he was a dead man. The king would have his head. On a platter. *For dinner!* He had *kissed* the dragon king's *sister!*

Everything made more sense now. The gold and bronze of her corseted gown—the colors of the royal family. The fact she hadn't said anything to him. How she spoke now was a mystery his panicked brain couldn't wrap itself around. Born without a voice, she had learned how to borrow the voices of other dragons, but it had to be a *dragon*. He was most definitely not a dragon. Maybe that part of her lore was wrong. Maybe she could use anyone's voice.

God, even her being held captive made sense.

The king of dragons loved his sister with a fondness that bordered on unnatural. She would have made the perfect leverage to move the king. He would have done anything to keep her safe. That is, if her kidnappers had managed to keep her imprisoned. Whoever chose her as their target had made several very grievous errors—one of which was underestimating Lady Carissa's power. With their escape, her kidnappers had just made the very top of the king's shit list.

Suddenly, his pants were less tight. The king would kill him, too, if he knew the kind of things Michael had been thinking about his sister.

Swallowing back his shock, Michael watched Carissa turn to take in the room. Her eyes seemed to be searching for something, but what? He looked around at all the enthralled humans. How he knew they were all human was beyond him at the moment, but he knew it. Her song grew in intensity. He could feel the magic searching for something. It brushed against his skin like a purring cat. A strangled sound drew his attention across the room as a single fellow crumpled to the floor, his strings cut. She had killed him with just her words. His eyes went back to his dragon lady. *Carissa*, he corrected in his mind. Lady Carissa, sister to the king. The most powerful dragon sorceress known to walk the earth. Her power rivaled even the king of dragons. Oh, he was so dead when they got out of here. Maybe Daniel could find him a nice hole to hide in for the rest of his natural life.

The strum of magic subsided as she brought her song to an end. Her voice was beautiful. Oh, how he would love to hear that voice, maybe a little hoarse, crying out his name in passion. He slammed that thought down with a quick reminder that she was the *king's sister*. But it did nothing to relieve the ache growing in his pants again. He was so going to die with blue balls.

He looked around the room at the men. All of them were crumpled to the floor, but the few he could see were still breathing, so they weren't dead. She had only killed the one man. Why not take them all out? It would solve a lot of issues.

There had been a rash of dragon disappearances, lately. After a long undercover operation, Michael had discovered this group. They had been kidnapping and killing dragons for their glands. The pheromones they produced sold for big money, but they couldn't be reproduced in a lab. It had been his own bad luck that had gotten him caught during his mission. If he hadn't gone back for that cup of coffee, he wouldn't have run smack-dab into their hands. Why they just hadn't killed him on the spot was still a mystery. Maybe they wanted to try to trade him for some of their buddies whom Daniel already had locked up. Fat chance there. Daniel didn't make deals. Anyway, Michael was an Elite. He was on his own.

His attention was pulled away from his thoughts when Carissa moved. Horror filled him as she crumpled to the floor. He tried to cry out her name, but his voice didn't work. She'd definitely stolen it to perform her trick. His heart squeezed when her form dissolved. Dragons only involuntarily shifted to their smaller forms in times of stress or need.

Voicelessly crying out her name again, he rushed to her side and dug the small, golden dragon from inside the body of the dress. He placed his hand on her side, feeling for a heartbeat. For a moment, he thought she was dead, and then she pulled in a raspy breath. His fingers finally located the staccato beat of her little heart—strong and steady. Michael let out a shaky breath as he cradled the limp dragon against his chest. If he'd had any questions about who she was, this cinched it. Only the royal family shifted into gold dragons. He stroked her head and tucked her wings in before turning to roll up her dress. She was going to need it as soon as she recovered.

Once everything was secure, Michael stood up and looked around. Getting her things together had been a quite a chore. He hadn't wanted to put her down in case he needed to get out of there fast. With her dress, rolled inside the corset, secured to his belt, and her jewels in his pocket, he looked around for the exit. There were three doors leading out of this room. Tucking Carissa into the crook of his left arm, Michael pulled out his gun and headed for the door on the right. He was taking no more chances with her safety.

Michael was surprised at how small Carissa was in this form. The gold dragons were the largest of the great dragon families. They towered head and shoulders above any of the other colors when in their great form. He had seen Carissa in that form many times. She was magnificent. The way the light sparkled off her scales always stole his breath away. Hell, the light sparkling off any color of dragon was magnificent. There was something in their scales that broke the light and reflected it back, like the prismatic coating on interstate signs. He had always wanted to touch her scales. They were so beautiful. His thumb rubbed gently against the side of her head where it rested in his palm. He looked down at her to make sure she was still okay.

God, she was so small. He had seen dragons in their little forms that rivaled Great Danes. But Carissa… she was barely the size of a house cat, although she did have a little length to her. With her head resting in his hand, the tip of her tail hung to nearly his knee. A scalloped frill covered her neck, but she lacked the horns her brother sported in his grander size. The tip of her tail ended in a fanning of soft strands. Not hair, but not hard like quills. It patted softly against his leg as he walked. For a second, the thought of that tail thumping into his back popped into his head. A shot of desire raced through him again. Oh man, he *had* gone crazy! Now he was having erotic thoughts about her in dragon form. That was just not normal. He had always loved the look of her as a dragon, but it had never caused him to lust before. He shook the thought away, readjusted himself, and worked his way down the next corridor.

Michael had been able to determine they were in some kind of castle-like building. The windows, if there were any, were small and set high in the stone wall. Some didn't even have glass in them. The halls all wound around oddly, like a maze. He had taken several wrong turns that came to dead ends, but he was able to avoid the people moving about. Carissa had rumbled a few times in her sleep but hadn't woken. He rubbed his thumb gently over her neck, hoping she would wake soon. He could really use her help to find a way out of here.

The sound of pounding feet echoed up the hall. Michael slipped into one of the side rooms so they could pass. Someone must have discovered the unconscious men in the barracks. Oh great, his job

just got harder. Michael considered finding someplace to hole up, but this group wouldn't stop searching for them until they had turned over every stone,
or found them. And with only one gun, he wanted
to be away as quickly as he could. A few minutes later,
a herd of feet thundered past, heading in the other
direction. He had to get out of there. Now.

Tucking Carissa tighter to his body, Michael
took off in a sprint down the hall away from where
he'd come. There had to be an exit around here somewhere. Something thumped against his back, causing him to whip around to find his attacker. Another
thump smacked him between the shoulder blades,
this time accompanied by a gurgle. He looked down
to find that he was squeezing Carissa hard against
him. He tried to curse and apologize as he loosened
his grip. She thumped him once more before climbing up his coat. Her needle-point claws bit into his
jacket before she wrapped herself around his neck.
Thank God for good leather.

"Can't find the way out," he mouthed to her
as she settled on his shoulders. She rubbed the top
of her head on his cheek soothingly before looking
around at their options. Noise was coming from behind them, so Michael started off down the corridor
again. When the hall dead-ended in the middle of
another, he stopped. Carissa thumped him hard on

the back with her tail and pointed her nose to the right. He turned right.

Every few steps, Carissa would swish her tail from the front of his body to the back. Movement to work out her nerves. God, he wished she would stop doing that. The soft thwap of the tufty bit at the end of her tail reminded him of that soft flogger his ex used to like. It really wasn't helping with his earlier thoughts. God, if he got out of this, got her safely back to the king, survived the king's wrath, then survived Daniel's wrath for his initial fuckup; he was so heading over to that BDSM club downtown. A pretty girl with a soft flogger would probably go a long way to work the dragon hormones out of his system. Carissa's tail thumped into his back again, and he caught the end when it came back around. She whipped her head around to look at him, but he just gave her a half smile and a shrug. It's not like he would explain the issue to her even if he could. Her tail stilled, but he held on, rubbing the soft fringe at the end.

Finally, natural light filled the far end of their hallway. Michael didn't care anymore; be it door or window, they were going to get out. Luck would have it that it was a door, a big, beautiful, wooden door being held open by a man. He was yelling something to someone outside, but that didn't bother Michael.

As soon as the man finished and went to shut the door, Michael smacked him in the back of the head with the butt of his gun. He dropped like a stone. A purr vibrated through his shoulder from Carissa. He shivered in response. Even while killing someone, just a sound from her made him hard.

What the hell was wrong with him? He had handled dragons before—heard their noises, felt their purrs, touched their scales—and none of them brought on any response even close to what she brought out in him. He wanted her. Right now. *In this form.* How was that even possible? He was going to need some serious counseling when the whole, sordid affair was over.

After a few deep breaths, Michael pulled himself together and opened the door. Two men turned to look at him. Two men. Michael could handle that. He pointed his gun at the first and pulled the trigger. The hammer fell on the round with an audible click, but nothing happened. A dud. He tried again, but the gun jammed up. *Shit!*

The men had frozen when the door had opened, but now they sprang into action. One raced away for help while the other came at them, fighting to get his gun out of wherever he had stuck it. Carissa launched herself at the man's face. Five pounds of teeth, claws, and wings distracted him enough for

Michael to shoulder-check him and smack them to the ground.

Carissa's wings and tail trembled and thrashed as she hissed from where she landed. Michael snapped the man's neck before turning to look at the little dragon. She didn't look hurt, but he was afraid she had gone down hard. He reached for her, but she snapped at him and turned towards the woods just beyond the courtyard.

Snapping to his senses, Michael looked around for the other man, but he was already out of sight. Dropping the useless gun, Michael chased after the flash of gold scampering across the open ground. She was quick for her size. Pausing at the tree line, Carissa waited long enough for him to catch up before slipping off into the woods. Chaos exploded from the castle behind them.

Snatching her up from the ground, Michael tucked Carissa back under his arm and booked it for all he was worth. He wasn't going to break any land-speed records, but he had trained for just this kind of thing. Sprinting short distances, he zigzagged his way through the trees, looking for a place to hide. Someplace to get away from the men he could hear following them. He shot for a break in the bush to his right. An unruly bramble caught his legs, and he slipped. Tumbling, he tucked Carissa in against his chest, protected by his arms. Who knew what kind of damage he could do to a small dragon if he fell on it. Panic filled him as he saw what they were falling towards. Nice, soft, green grass… at the bottom of a really long hill.

"*Let me go, you stupid man!*" Carissa hissed from where she was crushed to Michael's chest. Unfortunately, he didn't understand dragon. Didn't he have a brain cell in that head of his? She could have told him those brambles hid the edge of a cliff. Hadn't Daniel taught him *anything*? Didn't he know to release a dragon in a fall? Now he was going to crush her as they rolled down the hill. Oh yes, he had tucked her up between his arms to protect her body, but what about her wings or tail? What would happen if she broke something? Now that they were outside, it wouldn't take but a few moments for her to shift to a larger form and get them out of there, but he was too stupid to realize it. Just snatched her up and took off, willy-nilly, into the woods. God save her from men, no matter how they made her feel. And oh, how he had made her feel!

Waking up riding in his arms, even crushed to his chest while running, had been amazing. That was

definitely an experience she would like to try again—
in less hectic times, of course. Oh, and riding on his
shoulder, breathing in his warm scent. Sure, he could
definitely use a bath, but underneath, he had a rich
spice that tickled her nose. And on top of all that,
the wonderful musk of male dragon. Oh, she hadn't
expected that, at least not yet. The way he played
with the end of her tail had given her shivers like you
would not believe. How did he know that was one of
her sensitive spots? She wanted him. Right now—in
any form. Well, at least she had until the nutcase lost
his marbles and took off like a deaf bat.

Carissa let out a puff of angry air before
burying her head into Michael's chest. If they were
going to crash, she probably should do something
to ensure she survived enough to get them out of
this. Drawing in a deep breath, she pulled herself to
human form. And just in time, too. Michael shifted
his grip on her now-larger form and took the brunt
of the initial impact. It would have been nice to stop
there, but the incline of the hill decided they should
probably continue to the bottom.

Brush, sticks, rocks, and a plethora of other
poky things grabbed at them as they tumbled down
to rest on the nice, cool grass. At least *that* was slightly soothing. That fall would have been hell on her
wings. Surprisingly, they both survived unhurt. Well,
if you want to consider being scraped up on every

inch of exposed skin 'unhurt'. And she had a lot of exposed skin. Carissa threw off Michael's arms and launched herself to her feet. Their pursuers couldn't be far behind them. Turning on her companion, Carissa grabbed the front of the man's coat and pulled his face to hers.

"You stupid, stupid man!" she bellowed at him. "*Never* hold a dragon during a fall! *Wings* are *fragile!*" She slammed her lips into his, giving him back his voice. Throwing him back to the ground, she stormed into the open grass to change again. She was going to need a nap after this trip. And a steak… or two. Hell, she would probably eat a whole cow after this calamity of errors was through.

Carissa ignored Michael as she knelt down and shifted into her grand dragon form. She threw her head back in a silent roar as the power swirled through her. Now let's see him snatch her up and tuck her under his arm. Snickering to herself, she turned to find Michael had finally picked himself up.

Yells from the top of the ridge drew her attention. The bark of automatic gunfire split the air, and she pounced on Michael, snatching him up like he had done her. Two wingbeats, coupled with a great leap, had them both in the air. The gunfire sounded again as she circled, gaining altitude. Pointing her head towards the ridge, she let out a great blast of fire, roasting the three men pointing weapons at her. A heavy downdraft of her wings quenched the flames before they could catch on the trees. Her attackers were dead or dying; there was no need to burn down the entire forest in her anger.

Pointing her nose to the sun, Carissa pumped her wings. Oh, the feel of the wind against her scales. It had been too long since her last foray into the wild blue. She could really enjoy herself, if it weren't for the fool of a man screaming his damned head off. She should have kept his voice. Carissa glanced down to the prize in her front claws. So what if he hung upside down from pants that were starting to slip over his hips? There hadn't been much time to aim her pounce before taking off under gunfire. Okay, maybe there was a reason to be a little upset, but he should realize she wouldn't drop him. And so what if she did? She had plenty of altitude to catch him before he hit the ground. She was very agile on the wing.

Letting out a deep sigh, Carissa looked around for a safe place to land to adjust her hold on him. She could probably do it in flight, but she didn't want to risk popping him with her talons. He should just be happy she hadn't impaled him accidently while dodging bullets. Sure, they wouldn't penetrate her thick scales, but they still hurt like hell when they hit. A large, grassy field to her right looked promising, so she banked towards it

Chapter Four

MICHAEL'S THROAT WAS SORE BY THE TIME THEY alighted in a large cow pasture. Carissa had grabbed him around the waist when they'd left, but he had shifted during the sudden takeoff. He'd ended up dangling in a few sharp claws by his pants. Pants that were now precariously slipping. Hell, his ass was almost hanging out. Just the way he wanted to die—dropped from a dragon without pants. Right now, he could really use an erection. It might just save his life by holding his pants on.

Tumbling to the grass, Michael waited for the gusts of air to settle before glaring at the dragon. Anger coursed through him as he turned from her, undid his belt, and readjusted things. At least his pants weren't pressing into him uncomfortably anymore. He snickered to himself. This was one of the only times he had been completely soft around her. Safe on the ground, away from danger, and he was limp. Go figure.

Once properly dressed, he turned towards Carissa. She had stretched out on the grass with her front legs folded under her head, watching him. *Damn, did she check out his ass while it was hanging out?* He pushed that thought away and looked at her. Her magnificent wings were spread out, soaking up the warm rays of the sun. She was breathtaking. His heart skipped as desire reclaimed its hold on him. Now he knew he was really going insane. Desire for a reptile? Okay, so dragons weren't your typical reptiles, but still. That was like getting a hard on for an iguana!

He had always loved dragons. Even before the king came out and announced their existence, he had been fascinated with them. The way their scales twinkled, their power, their ability to fly. But, *never* had he *ever* lusted after one.

Channeling that lust into his anger, he yelled at her. "What the hell do you think you were doing?" Michael shook his fist at her. "Trying to kill me?"

She snorted at him but did not answer.

"Oh, so now you're the silent type." He crossed his arms and turned his back to her. He took a deep breath and tried to calm down. At least they were both alive and free. Something had to be said for that. A soft growl came from behind him. "Look." He turned to face her again. "I'm sorry I snapped.

I've had a really stressful week."

She snorted at him again.

"Okay, so we've both had a bad week. *God!*" He ran his fingers through his hair, trying to clear his mind. "All right." He let out a solid sigh and held his hands out to her. "Let's just leave it at 'I'm sorry, thank you, and you're welcome'. If we dwell on the details right now, we might start snapping at each other." His heart lightened when she snickered. "The real question now is—where are we?" He turned to look around. Maybe there was a town nearby. "I'm sure I can get Daniel to send a team to pick us up."

Carissa rumbled behind him.

Michael turned to look at her. She had crept closer to him as he surveyed the area. Damn, she was quiet for something so large.

Rumbling again, Carissa swung her head towards him. It was more than half his size, but still, it was beautiful. Michael's fingers ached to touch her. Giving in to his urges again, he closed the distance between them and ran his hand over her scales. Oh, they were so warm to the touch. His fingers tingled with pleasure. One large eye focused on him as he scratched his way down her cheek. It closed as he reached the edge of the boney frill at the back of her head. His finger slipped under the edge of the frill, exploring. When Carissa tilted her head to give him better access under the ridge, he took it. She purred as he scratched the skin up under it. His nail caught on a rough edge, and a single, gold scale skittered down her neck. Michael sucked in his breath. She was going to kill him for this. Michael picked up the fallen scale and held it up for her to see. "I'm sorry."

Carissa's eyes widened as they focused on the inch-and-a-half, shiny disk. She snorted and shook her head.

"Umm… How about I stick this in my pocket until we get to where we're going. Then you can have it back."

She eyed him warily before nodding her agreement.

Michael blew out a relieved breath as he slipped the scale into his pocket with her jewels. The loss of a single scale had turned Daniel into a paranoid freak for the months it took to grow back. Dragons were very protective of their hides; a single missing scale could leave a hole in a dragon's defenses. At least this one came from a protected area.

"How about we go see if we can find help?" Michael stepped away from her head, tucking his hands into his pockets. There was no way he was going to touch her again. "Let's try this way." He turned away from her and started walking across the field towards what looked to be a valley. If he walked far

44

enough, sooner or later they would come to some kind of settlement where they could get help.

Carissa growled behind him, stopping him in his tracks.

"No?" He looked back at her. "Then how about that way?" He pointed to the right.

She growled again.

He pointed in the other direction only to get another growl. Michael let out a deep sigh. "Look, I'm tired, I'm hungry, and I'm starting to get cranky. I'm sorry I messed up your scales. Why don't you just pick a direction, and I'll follow you."

Carissa glared at him.

There; he'd done it. He'd spoken his mind, and now she was just going to eat him. *Fine. Whatever.* It would solve a bunch of problems. When she didn't move, Michael dropped himself to the grass to brood. God, this wasn't him. He wasn't moody—for crying out loud, he was an Elite in Eternity! The years he spent in training made this little adventure look like a cake walk. Days on end with no sleep or food, hours of torturous drilling in all weathers, sometimes constant pain, and never once had he been accused of being moody. He was moody now.

Carissa glared at Michael. How dare he take that tone with her! Especially after pulling one of her scales off! Obviously, Daniel had made a grievous error in picking this man for Eternity. Out of hundreds of candidates, only the top ten percent were accepted into the organization. And of those, half washed out before seeing any type of duty. There was no room for attitudes in Eternity, but he was definitely having some kind of mood swing.

The truth of the matter smacked her in the face. He was having mood swings! Carissa studied the back of the brooding man. He had seemed level-headed when under fire, but now he was all over the place. Leaning forwards, she drew in a long breath of air, tasting him. Yup, his body chemistry was wacked out. She snickered, earning a glare from the temper-amental man.

This was rich! Carissa knew he would change but had expected it to take longer than this. She had already detected the rich sent of dragon musk from him, but now, now she could pick up the traces of brooding. Her good humor dried up fast. Oh God, that was just what this area didn't need: a full-grown, wild dragon in the heat of a first brooding! She had to get him somewhere safe. *Fast.*

Grabbing him up by the back of his jacket, Carissa flipped Michael over her head and down to the base of her neck. He cursed at her, but she ignored him as she sprang into the air. If he were smart, he would hold on. Another string of colorful words came out of him as he clung to her back. She beat the air into submission, gaining altitude. She knew this area. An old friend of hers had a mountaintop cabin somewhere around here. It should be far enough away from civilization to isolate him until his system balanced itself out. Oh God, what had she done? And she hadn't even had the chance to explain things.

Carissa pushed hard, searching for their destination. She could feel Michael's fingers clutch into her scales. Was he changing back there? She wanted to stop and check on him, but she was going to need help. Spying the mountain she wanted, she circled around until the high plateau came into sight. A thin steam of smoke rose from the small house nestled against the side of the mountain. Thank God someone was there.

Checking her speed, Carissa dropped them straight onto the front lawn. She shifted to human as soon as her feet touched, intending to run inside for help. The weight of the man on her back dropped her to the ground, instead.

"What the hell, woman?" Michael cursed at her.

Rolling in his arms, Carissa slammed her

mouth into his, silencing his protest. She had only intended to take his voice, but, unfortunately, it also drove his hormone levels straight through the roof. He groaned into her mouth and ground his pelvis into hers. His hands wandered over her skin, kneading, as he deepened their kiss. Heat pounded inside of her skull and drove splinters of desire through her body. Her heart pounded as he shifted above her. Oh, she was so wet. The touch of his hand against her core shocked her back to her senses. If she didn't do something soon, they were going to be rolling around, having wild monkey sex all over her friend's front yard for the next several days. In just a moment.

Moaning, she struggled to make herself stop him. But, he just felt so good. She gasped as his fingers slipped inside her. Twisting her head, she broke the kiss. His lips moved to the side of her neck instead. *Oh God!* He knew exactly how to touch a woman. Carissa's hands trembled as she moved them to his shoulders. Make him stop. Make him stop. Make. Him. Stop. The sound of a zipper ratcheted through her passion-filled senses. *Now!*

Pushing him hard, she flipped them over, so she was the one on top. Oh, to just stay right there. To have him put out the fire he had stoked. Hormones, she reminded herself. *He needs help!* She slammed a fast kiss to his lips and sat up. His hands caught her waist and pulled her against him, hard. Oh, to just let him have his way. It would be so easy. But, he wasn't in his right mind, and she couldn't take advantage of him. Could she? His hips had picked up a tantalizing rhythm. His lust-clouded eyes burned on her skin. No. She couldn't. No matter how much she wanted him to pound into her right this second. He wasn't in control. Gathering up everything she had, she slapped him as hard as she could and ripped herself from his grip. *Got to get help*, she scolded herself, forcing her wobbly legs to carry her into the house.

Chapter Five

OUCH! MICHAEL STARED UP AT THE FLUFFY PUFFS OF white floating in blue. What the hell just happened? His arms flopped out beside him, and he tried to get his brain to work. Apparently, only one head worked at a time. Probably lack of blood.

Shaking his head, he closed his eyes to focus. He had been sitting on the grass, brooding. He definitely remembered Carissa snatching him up, in her *mouth*, and tossing him onto her back. But what next? He didn't remember. Somehow, he went from clutching to her neck for dear life to her slapping him and running off.

He rolled his hand over and rubbed the vegetation. Nope, definitely different grass. So what had happened in between? Had they been having sex? It sure felt like it. He looked down his body. His clothes were all rumpled, and he could see himself, hard as a rock, sticking out of his open fly. Sure looked like it. There was an obvious sheen around his crotch where he had been rubbing up against something very wet. His body shuddered at the vague memory of soft skin under his hands. *What the hell?*

Sitting up, Michael pulled his coat off. It was too damned hot for it. He fluffed his shirt out, hiding his erection from view. There was no way he was going to stick that thing back in his pants right now. It hurt like hell. In fact, all of him ached. And why was it so damned hot! Where the hell were they?

He yanked the strings on his boots and kicked them off. If he couldn't get answers, maybe he could at least get comfortable. Ripping his socks off, he wiggled his toes into the cool grass. That was somewhat better. Sweat trickled into his eye. *But not good enough.* He yanked his shirt off and dropped it into his lap. *That's better.*

Lying back into the grass, Michael let his mind work on the problem. Was he sick? He ached. He was hungry. His mind was all over the place. A shiver hit him as the heat in the area disappeared. Okay, so maybe he was running a fever. And he *itched!* He wiggled his back into the ground, trying to scrape the skin off. *Definitely sick.* He was going to need to see the medic as soon as they got back. Then, straight to a psych eval.

God, he didn't want to lose his place as an Elite, but he couldn't go out on missions like this. He couldn't concentrate. Had that stay in a real dungeon cracked his mind? Or was it Carissa's hormones messing with his head? And who turned up the damned heat again?

Michael rolled onto his side, trying to find a position that didn't hurt and itch. Maybe he rolled through something as they fell down that hill. More memories popped into his head. The sight of Carissa storming away from him, naked and covered in scrapes. God, she was beautiful. His body pulsed with need. But, she was hurt. He had to find her.

Pushing up from the ground, Michael tried to call her name, but nothing came out. Damn it, she'd stolen his voice again. How did she do that? He managed to get to his hands and knees. Almost there. The heat disappeared from the world again. *Would someone please stop fucking with the thermostat?* It was really starting to piss him off.

He tried to push the rest of the way to his feet. Carissa was hurt. He had to find her! His limbs trembled as pain clenched his stomach. His hand shot to his middle, and he face-planted into the nice, hard ground. Great, definitely dying here. Someone tell his mother he loved her. He curled into a ball, groaning silently.

The shithead playing with the thermostat turned it up again… to about a thousand degrees.

God, his skin burned everywhere. Thrashing about, he ripped off his pants. Who cared if she saw him naked? At least those vile things weren't rubbing on his oversensitive skin. Now he just had to make it stop itching! Michael worked his nails into his arms, leaving long, bloody scrapes.

Another ball of pain shot out of his stomach. Curling his arms around his middle, he rolled into himself, face-down on the grass. He suddenly felt like he was coming apart at the seams. Maybe if he held on tight enough, he'd survive it. More pain raced down his back, leaving him silently screaming in agony. If anyone were going to kill him, now would be the perfect time. He would most definitely appreciate the relief.

One more agonizing breath, and his world shattered. He could literally feel his body rip itself apart. It shifted and swirled in on itself. God, he was going to be sick on top of everything else. Darkness closed over his eyes, and for one short, blessed moment, he was sure he was passing out. *Thank God.*

But he didn't. *Damn it.*

Seconds seemed to stretch on forever as alternating heat and cold tore their way through him. Couldn't his body make up its mind? Obviously not. Finally, after what seemed like eternity, the pain faded, the hot and cold decided to get together in a nice, comfortable warm, and the itching died to a dull roar.

Michael waited for the next bout of heat or pain, but it didn't come. Great. He'd survived. Yay. Now he just had to figure out what kind of bug he had caught so he could get the antidote.

He slowly opened his eyes. The world looked wrong. The colors were off. More brilliant. Sharper. He closed them again. Maybe he hadn't recovered yet. But, the world smelled different, too. Things he hadn't noticed before were sharper. The dirt and grass were divine. And he could smell her. Carissa. How he knew it was her was beyond him, but it was. And she smelled wonderful.

Mine!

His brain screamed out that one-word declaration. He had to find her. She was hurt. She was missing a scale. He had to protect her.

Pushing up, Michael managed to get to his hands and knees. Shit! His balance was way off. His body felt weird. Not hurt, just off. Carissa. *Mine!* He had to get to *Mine!*. She needed him. Opening his eyes, he took in the strange hues. God, that looked weird. Spying the cabin, he closed his eyes and followed his nose. She went that way. He just knew it. He staggered forwards on his hands and feet before toppling over onto his side.

Feet? How had he been on his hands and feet

without his butt being up in the air? It didn't matter right now. Protect *Mine!*. Michael tried to get up again but only managed to flop about on the ground. Darkness ate away at the edges of his mind. Great. Now that he had something important to do, he passed out. *Thanks world; I love you, too.*

"Darien!" Carissa screamed as she burst through the door. She paused for a moment as her eyes adjusted to the dim light in the cabin. Everything inside was still. Was he there? Her eyes found her quarry crouched on the floor in the corner, staring at her. He looked just as she remembered. Tall, trim, with twinkling green eyes.

Unfolding his lanky frame, Darien cocked his head at her. He ran his eyes up and down her naked body. "Carissa?" Setting the book he had been getting on the table, he crossed the room with an easy, flowing gate. "What's wrong?" He wrapped his long fingers around her shoulders and pulled her fully into the cabin.

Carissa pulled on Darien's long robes. "Come; he's changing."

Darien caught her hand and looked at the long scratches on her arms. He pulled in a deep breath. "Have you decided to take a mate?" His voice sounded intrigued.

A mate! How had he come up with that idea? Reality smacked her yet again. *Of course.* She was a mess; she smelled of male dragon, sex, and brooding. What other possible conclusion could he have reached? "No, no. Not that." Carissa shook her head. "It's just…" How was she supposed to explain this? She needed to get him out to check on Michael. "It's complicated. Come on." She pulled on his hand, trying to get the man to move.

"Carissa, My Lady, what happened?" He pulled her back.

Great. He was going to want the full story before he moved to help. She should have known; Darien never acted in haste. Fine, he wanted the story, he'd get it.

"I was kidnapped, thrown in a dungeon, mucked about with magic, and I escaped. Now there is a man out there in the process of changing into a dragon," Carissa rapid-fired at him. "Now, come on." She tugged at the immovable man's hand.

"You were kidnapped?" Concern filled his face and voice. "Are you hurt? Does your brother know?" Darien's hands tried to turn her around to check for wounds.

Carissa pushed them away. "I'm fine," she

snapped and regretted it. Darien didn't deserve the sharp side of her tongue. Man, she was frazzled. Taking a deep breath, she started again. "I'm sorry." Her voice was softer this time. "I got a little scraped up rolling down a hill as we escaped, but otherwise, I'm fine. I don't know if my brother knows; we just got out of there, and I haven't had the chance to talk to him. There is a man out front, Michael, in the middle of his first brooding."

"First brooding?" Darien's eyes widened. "Why would his mother let him out so close to a brooding? He could hurt himself."

"He's not a child." Carissa pulled on Darien's hand. "He's full-grown." Darien let her pull him forwards. *Finally!*

"Full-grown, and in a first brooding. How is that possible? Brooding starts around five or six."

"He's human. Or *was*." That got Darien's feet really moving.

"What have you done?"

"I needed a voice." Carissa's answer almost sounded like a whine. When had she started getting whiny? "Given the options, I made the only choice I could see." She looked over the yard for Michael. He was not where she had left him, but his clothes were. Where the hell had he gone?

"There are always options." Darien looked

over the mess strung across the yard. "Where's your friend?"

Panic rose in her heart. "I don't know." He could get into all sorts of trouble out there. He didn't know the first thing about being a dragon. Her eyes searched the scene. Coat, shoes, pants, shirt, underwear, *what's that white thing?* The form was familiar, but the color was wrong. Oh, God, no. Her feet carried her to it. Oh yes, a dragon, no larger than a house cat. Just like her small form, complete with the bony frill and fringed tail, but with little horns. Only, the color was all wrong.

Her brother was going to kill her.

Darien stood next to her, looking down at her problem. "Oh, Carissa, what have you done?"

"I woke up in a warded dungeon racked with pain," she explained as she reached down to touch the limp form. His heartbeat was steady. Good. "Michael was chained to the wall, dying. He's a trooper, but I could tell he wouldn't last much longer without water. So, I gave it to him the only way I could—by mouth."

Darien gave her a surprised look.

"Please don't lecture me. I'd just woken up, was in pain, on morphine, and, well, not thinking clearly."

"Obviously."

"Anyway, after that, he was in no state to help." Carissa gently rolled Michael over, tucking his wings back along his body. "I kept cursing myself. If I'd just had a voice, I could get us both out of there. Then it hit me. The old stories. Humans to dragons. If he were a dragon, I could use his voice to save us. I knew how it was done; many of my books spoke of it."

"They also spoke of the dangers," Darien chided her. "Carissa, his mind may not have survived the change. Humans are fragile creatures."

Carissa rolled the small dragon into her arms and held him close. "I know, but he's a member of Eternity." She stroked Michael's back.

Darien raised an eyebrow at her. "Are you sure?"

Carissa nodded at the clothing scattered around. "Their emblem was on his med pack. And his shirt."

"That doesn't mean a thing." Darien shook his head. "You know the differences between forms. It may be too much for his limited mind to handle. He could get stuck in one form, unable to change. Do you really want a mad dragon on a rampage?" His eyes held compassion as he spoke. "The best thing you can do is put him down, right now, before things get worse."

Carissa caressed the warm bundle as she

thought about it. It would be easy. Just a quick twist of that tiny head and *snap*, no more problems. But what kind of way was that to repay him for his service? Without his help, she would still be in that cell. He had carried her to freedom when she passed out. He had done everything he could to protect her. Now she was supposed to kill him for his kindness? She ran her fingers over the white scales. No, not white. Clear. Carissa bent closer to him. His scales had the same iridescence of any dragon, but they lacked the pigment that gave them color. Interesting.

"No," she decided. "I'll deal with it if he's lost," she turned her eyes up to Darien, "but he at least deserves a chance."

"As you wish, My Lady." Darien crossed his hand to his heart and bowed to her, accepting her decision. "I am at your service."

Great, now Michael had his own personal executioner. Woo-hoo. Things were not going as well as she planned. Well, she hadn't really planned *anything*, but still.

"Thank you, Darien." She cuddled the little dragon to her again. "I hope to never have to call on your services for that."

"Why don't we get you both inside?" Darien held his hand down to help her up. "It sounds like you've had a trying time. Maybe some food would help."

That was the best idea she had heard since waking up. "Sounds great."

Chapter Six

MMM.... SOMETHING SMELLS WONDERFUL. SUCKING IN a deep breath, Michael savored the smell of cooking meat. An undertone of something musky hit his nose, making him sneeze several times. The meat he liked; the second smell raised his hackles. Opening his eyes, Michael looked around for the source of that second smell. God, the world still looked weird. Maybe he had hit his head.

It took a little bit of time, but his brain finally figured out how to process the imagines his eyes were sending. The inside of a cabin. Built for giants. Or maybe a grand dragon. Yes, he could see some eccentric, old dragon building himself a cabin where he could play human in dragon form. A wizened, old thing, with long, flowing robes, reading dusty tomes through thick spectacles. Yup, that was it. He had a puzzle with that image on it somewhere. And this room fit the bill.

From his vantage point—someone had put

him on the floor—the room looked right out of some Renaissance movie. A great hearth filled the center of one wall, and bookcases lined the rest. A large, wooden table with four chairs towered over him to the left, and a mountain of a bed was just to his right. That smell seemed to come from everything. He stuck his nose into the blanket wrapped around him and sneezed. Yes, that reek was definitely from whoever lived here. He had to get out of here.

Wiggling from the blanket, Michael managed to get up on his hands and knees again. Standing all the way up seemed beyond him for the moment. His body still felt odd. Maybe he just needed to get out and stretch.

Michael pulled himself out onto the wooden floor. Someone had used massive trees to make these boards. Cool air spilled across his skin. Was he naked? Closing his eyes, he tried to recall where he was. Yes, he remembered the frantic tearing off of clothing. If someone had brought him inside, maybe they had brought his clothes in, too. It would have made the most sense to leave them by his bed.

Turning back, his eyes scanned the pile of blankets he had used. No clothes, but there was something white sticking out of the blankets. It looked fluffy, but not like hair. He had seen something like that before, but he couldn't remember what. Curiosity crawled through him. He just had to find out what that was. Carefully, he crawled towards it. An itch hit him on the back of the neck, and he shivered.

Michael froze as the white thing twitched. Was it alive? He was almost to it. One good lunge and he would have it. Bunching up his muscles, he sprang forwards with all his might, grabbing at the thing with his mouth. *Mouth?* Why was he using his mouth? The thought skittered out of his mind. All he had to do was chomp down, and he would have it. God, he wanted that thing!

Just as Michael's jaws tightened on the fluffy thing, a pain shot up his tailbone. Michael stifled the yelp that would have released his prize and rolled away from the blanket and whatever was causing him pain.

A long, snakelike thing was attached to the fluffy, white thing. Recognition hit him. That was a dragon tail. He had a dragon by the tail! He spit the tuft out and spun to face the dragon he had just bitten, but the tail skittered away from him. Where was the dragon? He spun farther, looking for it. How could the thing hide? It had to be as big as he was.

Michael froze. Something wasn't right. The tail was white. There were no white dragons. His brain wasn't working right, but he knew his dragons. He looked over at the white, tufty thing. Carefully shifting his eyes, he followed the tuft to the tail and up to his backside. Wait, he didn't have a tail. Turning his head farther, he followed the white scales up his side to the neatly folded wings on his back. No, no, no, this was not happening!

Michael whipped his head back to the room around him. Was he dreaming? When he was a kid, he used to dream he was a dragon. A grand, green dragon. But it had been years since he'd had those dreams. God, he had to find a mirror or something reflective. He *couldn't* be a dragon; he was human.

Scampering across the room on legs that were much too dragon-like, Michael frantically searched for something reflective. A flash of gold caught his eye—a polished plate. Oh, yes, that would work nicely. Closing his eyes, he crept up on it. This was just a dream. He was not really a dragon. Cracking an eye, he looked at the reflection. Yup, dragon. Closing his eyes again, he shook his head. *I am not a dragon.* He tried to speak the words into being true, but nothing came out. Hoping it worked anyway, Michael opened his eyes again. Still a dragon.

A male voice from the doorway caught Michael's attention. That musky smell was getting stronger. What if this man had done something to make him a dragon? Was he friend or foe? Suspicion shot through him, and he bolted for the darkness under the bed. *Must hide. Can't be caught.* Maybe he could get out of the cabin while the man wasn't looking. Then he would find his way to Daniel. Daniel would know what to do.

"It will take the birds several hours to reach your brother," the man's voice said.

Michael suppressed the hiss rising in his throat. He did not like this musky man.

"Why don't you sit down and have something to eat? The stew should be about done." The man crossed to the hearth, where a pot hung over the fire.

Now would be a great time to bolt for the door. It was open, but he couldn't tell who the man was talking to.

"Sure," a woman's voice answered.

Michael froze. He knew that voice. She was important. One of the chairs at the table scraped out. A scent hit him as she sat down. *Mine!* He crept out so he could see her. Carissa. Memories slammed into him. She was hurt. She was missing a scale. He had to protect her. She was sitting in a room with a man that may have turned him into a dragon! All sense ran out of him as instinct kicked in.

Michael launched himself out from under the bed and scrambled up the side of the chair and onto the table. Dragon claws rocked for climbing. He placed himself between Carissa and the man, fanned out his wings, and hissed at the danger in the room. He would protect her with his life!

"Why don't you sit down and have something to eat?" Darien said as he stepped through the door. "The stew should be about done." He crossed over to check on the bubbling pot.

That was the best idea of the evening. Now that messages had been sent to all the possible places her brother could be, Carissa could relax. And why hadn't Darien joined the twenty-first century? Was a phone too much to ask? How about a normal stove, at least?

"Sure," Carissa answered. Tucking up her borrowed robes, she pulled out a chair and sat down. Maybe she should check on Michael before she ate. The poor man was not having a very good day. The sound of claws on wood grabbed her attention just before a flash of white blocked her vision.

Carissa and Darien both froze. Five pounds of angry dragon quivered on the table between them, hissing at Darien. At least Michael was awake and moving.

Slowly, Darien stood up from the pot and looked at the dragon, checking out his posturing.

The tips on Michael's wings rustled in warning.

Darien smiled at Carissa. "Definitely brooding." He lowered his face until he was eye-level with Michael. "Listen, little one, I'm older and bigger than you, so calm down."

Carissa rolled her eyes as Michael hissed again. "Stop antagonizing him." She slipped her hands up under Michael's wings to hold him back. His muscles were all bunched up, ready to attack. "It's all right, Michael," she said, trying to soothe him.

The little dragon's tail thrashed back and forth as he stared Darien down.

If she didn't do something fast, he was going to launch himself at Darien. Oh, that would make a fine mess of this already-fine mess. The end of his tail thwapped into her arm, and she grabbed it up. She stuck the fringy end in her mouth and chomped down.

Michael jerked in a silent yelp and twisted to glare at her.

Oh, that got his attention. "Michael!" Carissa snapped. "Down, now!"

The little dragon froze.

She hated ordering him around like that, but he was out of control. His crystal-blue eyes were more feral than anything. Had she made a mistake not killing him while he was asleep? Please let him be all right. "Please calm down. Everything's fine. You're safe." She watched the wheels turn in Michael's head. Please, oh please let him be in there.

A snarl curled Michael's lip as he turned back to look at Darien.

"That's Darien. He's here to help."

Michael tuned back to look at her again. His mind still processed her words, but he tucked his wings down.

Well, that was at least a start.

"It looks like he may retain at least part of his mind," Darien commented. "But, will it be enough?"

Carissa looked at the little dragon. He was studying her with confused eyes. "He's in there." God, she hoped he was in there. "Just give him a little time. He just woke up." She reached out and rubbed his cheek.

Michael closed his eyes and leaned into her touch.

She didn't want to think about what she would have to do if he weren't home anymore.

Darien nodded at her. "As you wish, My Lady."

Great, there was that executioner again.

"How about if I get you both some food?" Not waiting for an answer, Darien turned back to ladle the stew into bowls.

Carissa wrapped her hands around Michael and drew him closer. "Darien's bringing food." She spoke softly to him, praying he understood her. "Just stay calm. We'll get through this together."

The little dragon cocked his head, processing her words. Slowly, he nodded his head.

Yes! He understood her. Carissa wanted to snatch him up and dance around the room, but she settled for rubbing her thumbs along his sides. Questions floated in his eyes. They were much clearer then they had been. "I know you have questions," that had to be the understatement of the century, "but, let's get food first. Then we'll see about getting you back to human form to ask them."

Michael nodded more quickly this time.

Thank you, God. Things might actually work out.

"I would suggest you both sleep before he tries to shift." Darien set two bowls and a plate of stew on the table. "You're both exhausted. He would have a much better chance of reaching human form if he were fully rested."

Michael rumbled a little at the man's voice.

Carissa caressed him reassuringly. "True," she agreed. Darien did have a valid point. She looked down at the little dragon between her hands. "Food first, then a nap. And I promise that we'll get you back to human when we wake back up."

Michael considered her for a moment before nodding his agreement.

Great! She could really use a nap. Maybe after a nice nap, he might be able to forgive her for ruining his life.

Chapter Seven

FRIEND. THE MUSKY-SMELLING MAN WAS A FRIEND. Michael shook his head; his brain wasn't working right. Darien. *Mine!* had called him Darien. No, that wasn't right, either. Her name was Carissa. She was important, but how? God, if she would just stop rubbing him, he might be able to think. Oh, but it felt so good.

Food. She mentioned food. The smell of cooked meat hit him like a Mack truck. Now he remembered—it had been the smell of food that had woken him up. Turning around in Carissa's hands, he saw the musky smelling man… A growl rose in Michael's throat, but he caught it. No. Darien. Friend.

Darien pushed a plate of chunks towards him.

"It's okay, Michael. Eat." *Mine!* patted him… Wait, that wasn't right. Carissa. *Carissa* patted him on his sides.

God, he wanted to eat that. It looked so good. Michael turned his eyes back for reassurance. He

wanted to eat, but he didn't trust the musky man…
no, Darien. *Mine!*… no, Carissa nodded encouragingly. He inched towards the plate cautiously. Brown,
orange, and white in brown stuff. The savory smell
made his mouth water.

Snatching up a hunk of meat, he backpedaled to the edge of the table in front of *Mine!*. He
had to protect her from that man. No, wait. Carissa didn't need protecting. Darien was a friend. She
trusted him. Michael could smell that she trusted
him. Oh, this whole thing was confusing. Michael
tried to chew the oversized hunk of meat. It didn't
work. He dropped it to the table to rip off a smaller
bit.

"Here, let me help you." *Mine!*… no, Carissa.
Carissa drew the plate closer to him and used a fork
to cut the chunks up into tiny bites.

That was better. Michael licked up the gravy
from the table and stalked up to the plate again.

Darien watched him closely from the other
side of the table.

Darien! Yay, he didn't have to remind himself
of the man's name. But, Michael still didn't like him.
Something about that musky smell rubbed him the
wrong way. Carefully, Michael pulled up an orange
hunk. Carrot. He liked carrots. Next, a white chunk.
Potatoes. Oh, potatoes were good. Especially in stew.

Yes, this was beef stew. But something was missing. Michael licked at the thick liquid. No, gravy. He licked at the gravy. Michael looked around, working his mind. A pepper mill! Yes! This needed *pepper!*

Ignoring both sets of eyes watching him, Michael weaved his way across the table to the pepper mill. It was huge! How was he ever going to get that thing back to his plate, or even use it? Wait, he wasn't alone. He could ask *Mine!*... no, Carissa. He could ask Carissa to put pepper on his food. Looking up at her, Michael found her watching him. He opened his mouth to ask, but nothing came out. *Crap!* Looked like he'd have to get it himself.

Rubbing his shoulder up against it, Michael knocked the mill towards the center of the table. Thankfully, it missed most of the stuff there.

"It looks like your friend wants pepper." Darien smiled at Carissa. "Would you like help?"

Michael froze in his efforts to shove the mill across the table with his head. Did he want help? Yes, but did he want Darien's help? The man still raised his hackles. *Mine!*... no, Carissa trusted him. He drew in a deep, calming breath and sneezed from the pepper. Breathing at the wrong end of a pepper mill was bad. He cleared his nose and looked up at Darien. The man had an eyebrow raised, waiting for an answer. Michael nodded his head and gave the pepper mill one last push with his front paw.

"Of course." Darien chuckled as he picked up the mill and turned it a few times over Michael's plate.

Oh, that looked so good. Michael started back to his plate. The smell of something else stopped him halfway across the table. To his left. A basket. There was a bundle of cloth holding something. Warm yeast rolls. That would just make the stew better. Michael stuck his head in and pulled out a roll larger than his head. Dropping it on the table, he backed across the table, dragging the thing. God, it tasted good.

Gold flashed in the corner of his eye. Carissa. She was just sitting there, watching him with the roll. Maybe she wanted one, too.

Manhandling the roll across the table, Michael staggered under the weight as he carried it to her. He dropped it next to her bowl before going back to get another for himself. His mother had taught him to always serve others first. He pushed the second roll to his plate. There, that was better. Circling around the dish, he settled so he was facing the middle of the table. It would be rude to eat with his back to everyone.

Beef stew with pepper and a warm yeast roll. The only thing that would make this better would be a pint of beer. Oh well. Michael tipped his head and said grace over his plate. He wasn't religious, but his mother would have skinned him for not being thankful for his food. That done, he dug into the first meal he'd had in days. God, that was good.

***

He brought me a roll! Carissa looked down at the teeth marks in the bread next to her bowl and nearly cried. That simple act could have meant many things. Was it instinct, providing for a possible mate? Her mind flickered to the memories of them out on the lawn, and heat pooled low in her gut. She could see how a brooding dragon might consider her a mate. Was it good manners? She looked over at the little dragon eating his plate of stew with pepper. He had remembered things like seasoning and rolls. That showed some signs of humanity. Reaching out, Carissa ran her hand over Michael's back.

The little dragon turned to look at her with questioning eyes.

"Thank you," she said softly.

Michael cocked his head to the side, showing confusion.

"For the roll."

He nodded his head and turned back to

his meal. When he ripped a hunk of bread off and dropped it into the gravy, her heart leaped. She hadn't lost him. He was in there. Thank you. Thank you. *Thank you.* Now all she had to do was teach him what he needed to know.

"Looks like my service won't be necessary. I'm glad." Darien smiled from the other side of the table.

There, the beheading sword was truly put away now. Those few, simple acts proved that Michael could be redeemed. Carissa hadn't condemned the poor man to die with her momentary lack of reasoning. He had even let Darien help him with the pepper. Darien—a mature, male dragon. A possible rival for a mate. Even Carissa could smell the increase in pheromones Darien was producing in response to a brooding dragon in his space. And Michael had agreed to his help. Oh, happy days! Elated, Carissa turned back to her stew and ate.

It took her and Michael no time at all to plow through two servings each. How he had stuffed all that food in that tiny body was unfathomable, but his little tummy bulged happily when he had finished licking the gravy from the bowl. Stuffed to the brim, full and content, Michael rolled onto his back next to his plate and let out a burp that made Carissa smile. He was just so cute.

Unable to help herself, Carissa rested her

head on her arms and reached out to that fat, little belly. It was just screaming to be rubbed. He was so soft and warm under her finger. She scratched absentmindedly while the fringy bit of his tail patted her leg rhythmically. So comfortable, so content, she could just… Carissa started back to awareness at the sound of Darien's chair pulling out.

"Why don't you go lie down," he nodded to the bed in the corner, "before you fall asleep at the table." Darien stood up and stacked the dishes together.

Carissa nodded and forced herself to stand up. She scooped Michael up like a baby, causing him to rumble unhappily. A few, soft tummy rubs soothed him back to his semiconscious state. "Thank you, Darien." Carissa nodded to her friend. "I owe you for this." She slipped into the bed and settled Michael next to her.

"It's no problem, My Lady." Darien came over and pulled the covers up over her properly. "You are always welcome in my home."

Carissa smiled at him sleepily.

"In a while, I have to head out for a bit, but I shouldn't be long. You're safe here."

She nodded her understanding as sleep crept up and stole over her. Finally, a chance to really rest.

Chapter Eight

WAP. WAP. WAP. NOISE CUT INTO CARISSA'S DREAM. Who the heck was making that horrible racket? Dragging herself from sleep, she shifted over to her side. Michael's warmth snuggled into her back as she stared at the doorway through cracked eyes. Her brain worked on the sound. It was something she had heard before. The high whine of machinery shutting down had her sitting up. A helicopter. Who would bring a helicopter up here?

She stopped breathing as a black-clad man with a gun pushed through the door. It took her a moment to recognize the uniform. Eternity! He brother was here! Relief flooded through her. She opened her mouth to speak, but nothing came out. Shoot. The magic she had used to borrow Michael's voice had worn off. Oh well, they wouldn't expect her to talk to them, anyway. She waved a hand in greeting.

"She's here." The man spoke into a mic

mounted on his shoulder. His eyes swung across the room, searching. "Negative on the target."

Carissa tipped her head over, making her confusion obvious.

The man circled around the inside of the cabin, looking in every possible nook and cranny. "All clear here." He stopped at the foot of the bed and turned his back to the wall to watch the room. There was a tension in him that Carissa did not like.

"Carissa!"

A voice pulled her attention from the guard. The king stepped through the door in all his glory. Surprisingly, his 'glory' consisted of jeans and a wrinkled T-shirt. Man, he was dressing down today. He paused just inside the door, scanning the room as the guard had.

"Are you all right?" her brother asked as he finally crossed the room to her. "He didn't hurt you, did he?"

Carissa stood up and hugged her brother. With his golden hair rumpled and dark bags under his amber eyes, Carissa was sure he hadn't slept since she had gone missing.

Kyle's hands ran up and down her back, looking for wounds. He leaned away and looked into her eyes. "Please tell me he didn't hurt you."

Carissa smiled and shook her head. Other

than a few scrapes, she was fine.

"Thank God." Kyle drew her in for another hug before pulling her down to sit on the edge of the bed. "I was so worried when I got Darien's message. How dare that man have the audacity to come here after what he put you through!"

Carissa looked at her brother with confusion. Who did what?

Ignoring her unvoiced questioned, Kyle touched her arm again as if confirming that she was really safe. "So, where is he?" The king's eyes shifted from her to search the room again. The same, nervous tension in the guard rode her brother, too.

There was something they weren't telling her. Carissa grabbed Kyle's arm, forcing him to focus on her. *Who?* she mouthed at her brother. She was pretty sure they were looking for Michael, but something was not sitting right with her. This was not a man looking forward to meeting someone who had saved his sister. He was obviously angry about something.

"Michael Duncan." Kyle growled the name. "I promise that he will pay for what he's done."

Red flags waved in warning. Something was definitely not right. *Why?* Carissa mouthed again, confused. What had Michael done? Her hand slipped down to cover the little lump of dragon next to her on the bed. He hadn't moved since she'd gotten up.

81

Hopefully, he would remain asleep until she could figure out what was going on.

"He's responsible for your kidnapping, among other things."

A pain shot through Carissa's chest at her brother's words. She clutched at the blanket over Michael. How could that be? He had been chained up in the dungeon. He'd helped her escape. Carissa shook her head emphatically, denying her brother's words. She could not—*would not*—believe that Michael had had anything to do with her abduction.

"It's true." Kyle smoothed his hand over her arm, trying to calm her. "We have him on video carrying you out of the ball."

Carissa gave him a distressed look. Could it be true? Had Michael helped in her kidnapping, and then the group chained him up in the dungeon? But he had killed at least two of them. He didn't seem heartless enough to turn on his own people, but, then again, she hadn't known him for very long. Was it possible?

Tears clung to the edges of Carissa's eyes. Michael's betrayal stung her heart more deeply than she cared to think about. Her fingers gripped tighter into the material under her hand. All she had to do was rip the covers back to reveal the little dragon snuggled in the warmth she had left. She'd have to explain his form to her brother, but he would take care of the man. Kyle would see that he got the punishment he deserved.

Deserved… That word hung heavy in her mind. Had Michael really done what her brother said? She had to know. If she gave him over to her brother now, she would never get the chance to confront him. It's not like he could just transform back to human and answer her questions. She needed time alone with him.

Carissa looked back up to her brother's concerned eyes. He was waiting for her to come to terms with reality. Carissa nodded her head. She would accept his word for now. He drew in a breath to comfort her but was interrupted by someone at the door.

"Pardon me, My King," Daniel raised his hand to his heart and bowed when he stopped in the doorway. "The perimeter's secure, but there's no sign of Michael. I suggest we get Lady Carissa to safety. I'll leave a squad here to search for him."

"Very good." Kyle stood up from the bed and held his hand out for Carissa.

Oh, God! She had to do something fast. She couldn't leave Michael here. Daniel's men would find him. But how was she supposed to get him out with Daniel and her brother there? She took her brother's hand and stood up as she thought. Kyle pulled her over and wrapped his arm around her to escort her out. This was not going well.

A flash of gold and bronze caught Carissa's eye as Kyle led her to the door. Her gown! Michael's coat was folded under it. Carissa pulled against Kyle's arm as inspiration struck.

"What?" Kyle looked down when Carissa resisted him.

She held out the front of her borrowed robes and pointed to her dress balled up next to the bed.

He looked from her to the bundle, then back to the man following them. "Get Carissa's things." Kyle tried to lead her on to the door as their guard bent to gather up her dress.

Carissa threw off her brother's hand and backed away from him, shaking her head.

Kyle looked at her, concerned.

She held up the borrowed robes.

"We can return Darien's robes later."

Carissa shook her head adamantly and took the bundle of her clothing away from the guard.

Kyle pinched the bridge of his nose and took a deep breath. "Fine," he agreed. "Do you need a hand getting dressed?" When Carissa shook her head, he ushered everyone else out so she could change. "You have five minutes. Bang on something if you need help."

Letting out the breath she'd been holding, Carissa quickly shook out her dress. Darien would have gladly let her keep his robes, but this was the only way to get the men out of the room. Slipping into the horribly wrinkled dress, Carissa grabbed up Michael's coat. What the hell did he have in those pockets? It weighed a ton. Ignoring the weight, she slipped it on and zipped it part of the way up. Using the strap at the waist, she cinched the bottom closed. The leather puffed out around her slight frame. Perfect.

Flipping back the blanket, she snatched up the sleeping dragon and fed him into the jacket. Michael squeaked as she stuffed him in. Carissa shushed him as she rolled up his tail and tucked it in, too. Her brother would be back in if she didn't hurry up. She patted his bulk as she turned to head out. It was the best she could do. Now, she just had to pray it worked.

What the hell, woman? Michael tried to yell, but it came out as a garbled, squeaking noise. Waking up to someone stuffing you inside a jacket was not his idea of a good morning.

Carissa shushed him as she pushed him the

rest of the way in and zipped up his jacket.

His jacket! What was she doing wearing his jacket? Michael shook his head and crawled around her back in the bulge the oversized coat made around her middle. At least she belted the bottom tight so he wouldn't fall out.

"Are you ready?"

The muffled voice made Michael freeze. He recognized that voice. Oh, God! The king was here! Now he was really going to be in trouble. But why had Carissa stuffed him down inside his jacket? Carefully, he crawled up the inside of the coat, trying to see out. Pressure stopped his movement. Was she holding him down?

"Isn't that Michael's jacket?"

That voice Michael knew well. Daniel! He wiggled to get out. He needed to see Daniel. The pressure increased, holding him away from his goal. What was Carissa thinking? He needed out.

"We'll need to take that in for evidence."

This comment from his boss made Michael freeze. He felt Carissa clutch at the jacket protectively. What was going on out there?

"Please, My Lady," Daniel continued. "It may have leads to his whereabouts. We need to find him as soon as possible."

Carissa held the pressure on him so he

couldn't move.

"Just leave her be." The king's voice came from just above Carissa's shoulder.

Michael felt his arm press into the leather as he drew Carissa into a protective hold.

"I'm sure she's having a hard enough time as it is. I'll get you his damned coat later."

Michael shivered at the anger in the king's words. Something was definitely not right.

"But, it might help us find him," Daniel pressed. "He never goes anywhere without that thing. He's damn good, and we need every edge we can get if we are going to stop him before he strikes again."

What?

"Just leave it," the king growled.

Michael clung to the inside of his jacket as he processed the conversation. What did they think he was doing?

The gentle swaying of Carissa's body told him they were moving again, but where were they going? Michael hated not being in control. Listening closely, he could hear the high-pitched whine of a helicopter starting up. Carefully, he inched up so he was pressed between his jacket and Carissa's chest in an attempt to see out. Michael could just see Daniel through Carissa's fingers. She had raised her hand in an attempt to keep him hidden inside the coat. Daniel looked pissed.

Normally, Daniel was a fairly easygoing individual. Something really bad had to have happened for him to be that angry. Inching back down, Michael tucked himself in against Carissa's stomach to listen. Maybe he could find out what was going on. The noise from the helicopter made eavesdropping difficult until they were tucked away inside the soundproof interior.

"It's not something you should be worrying about, My Lady."

Daniel's words made Michael freeze again. What had Carissa asked him? God, Michael wished she had a voice. It would make eavesdropping so much easier. The tuft of his tail smacked him on the nose as he fidgeted, waiting to hear more. Chomping down on a few of the tassel-like ends, he worried them with his teeth in an attempt to keep from bolting from the coat and demanding to know what was going on.

Carissa shifted as if she were talking with her hands.

"Truly," Daniel tried again, "I'm sure you don't want the details."

Carissa made a sharp motion that made Michael bite down on his tail a little harder.

"Just tell her." The king's voice came from

somewhere to Carissa's right. "You know she won't stop until you do."

Michael chuckled at Daniel's exasperated sigh. Obviously, this was not something he wanted to go into.

"I still can't believe it was Michael." Defeat was strong in Daniel's voice. "And to think, he actually volunteered."

Michael spit out his tail. There was only one assignment he had volunteered for recently. That was chasing down the persons responsible for the dragon disappearances. No, they couldn't think he was involved with that… could they?

"As I'm sure you've heard, about a year ago, dragon pheromones started showing up in clubs around the country." Daniel's voice was heavy. "We originally thought it was a group of dragons looking to make some extra cash, but the stuff was extremely concentrated. So, we started digging. We were able to link several missing dragons to the pheromones being sold. All the dragons had the same M.O.: loners, like Darien. Ones that only ventured out when they had to. It must have been months before we realized dragons were being targeted. I sent out men to check on as many as we could. God, I was amazed at how many were missing. Ten in this area alone." Daniel let out an angry growl.

"Michael and his partner, Jareth, volunteered to head up the investigation. They were to look for any suspicious activity. A week ago, Jareth sent me a report of everything they had found. Stories and eye-witness testimonies of the missing dragons' doings.

"There wasn't much to go on, but several people claimed to have seen Michael with a few of the dragons just before they disappeared."

Michael squirmed inside the jacket. He wanted to scream. That's not what they had found!

"He's also one of the few people with access to the solitary dragons list. I had Jareth looking into Michael's recent activities. Apparently, Michael made several trips in the last few months, right around the time the dragons disappeared."

Michael thrashed in anger.

Carissa's arms came down, squishing Michael into her body, holding him still.

"At that point, Michael hadn't sent in a report, but he was always one to check his facts carefully and present them in person. I was going to question him when he came in. Everything Jareth found was circumstantial, and I had a hard time believing Michael could be involved with these abductions. I've known the man for a damn-long time." Daniel let out a forlorn sigh before continuing. "Then Michael disappeared, too. Jareth said he went to get some coffee and never came back.

"I wanted to believe that he had a reasonable explanation. Then you disappeared." The tone of Daniel's voice got bleaker, if that were even possible. "I spent hours going over the video surveillance from Baron Estivis' ball. I couldn't believe it when I saw him come out carrying you."

Michael squirmed against Carissa's still form. He wanted to thrash someone. How could they make her believe he was responsible for her abduction? Her heart rate and breathing had gone up drastically. The coat puffed out as she squeezed her arms into the sides of the leather. Michael stretched to see her. Tears streamed from her eyes as she looked down at him. Hurt hung on every part of her beautiful face.

Reaching a clawed foot up to touch the front of her corset, he met her accusing stare. *No!* Shaking his head, he tried to convince her of his innocence. He had not done what they were claiming. He wanted to boil out of his hiding spot and deny the accusations, but he didn't have anything to offer as proof. Carissa's hands over the leather convinced him to remain where he was.

A wave of golden hair hid her face from everyone else as she considered him. She sniffed back tears before raising her head and nodding towards where Daniel must be seated.

God, she had made some decision for him, but what was it?

"Don't worry, Carissa," the king tried to calm his sister. "Justice will be quick for him."

Shit! That sounds like a royal decree! Had they already sentenced him without hearing his defense? Carissa must have picked up on the same note. Her back had gone very rigid.

"No, no. We haven't sentenced him yet."

Carissa must have mouthed something to him.

"He'll be given a proper trial if he turns himself in, but I have authorized Eternity to use force if he resists."

Oh, crap!

"He's an Elite, after all," Daniel added.

Well, thank you, boss! Michael chomped back down on the tip of his tail to keep from growling. He could just see how this was going to turn out. If it had only been the disappearances, he might have had a chance by turning himself in and fighting the charges, but Carissa's kidnapping had ensured that the Elites would shoot first and ask questions later. He was as good as dead.

Chapter Nine

"ARE YOU SURE YOU'RE OKAY?"

Carissa pushed her brother's hands away and took off to her private quarters without answering him. She needed to get away from everyone. She could feel Michael wrapped around her middle. He had let out a constant string of angry rumbles since Daniel had finished. Thankfully, the noise of the helicopter had drowned out the sound. Didn't that man know the first thing about hiding? Had his coat been any tighter on her, his constant fidgeting would have been a dead giveaway. She was going to have words with him as soon as she could speak again.

Slamming her door shut, Carissa yanked open Michael's jacket and dumped him out on her bed.

He rolled around in a tangle of wings before righting himself and chattering at her angrily.

Like he had any right to be angry! She had protected him from her brother and Daniel. If he had done *any* of the things they had accused him of, then she was going to be in a world of trouble. She was already going to get it for turning him into a dragon.

Carissa watched as Michael paced laps around her bed, chittering on. He was really worked up about something. Too bad he hadn't figured out how to speak dragon. Then she might have been able to tell if Daniel's story held any grains of truth.

Suddenly, he stopped and turned to her with imploring eyes.

What could he want? Carissa sighed and sat on the edge of the bed. Oh, what she wouldn't give to be able to just crawl into bed and go back to sleep. Carissa tried not to think about the few hours of rest she had just gotten. It had been so nice cuddled up with Michael, even as a dragon.

Michael came over and rested his front claws on her leg.

Her hand settled over his back to stroke him soothingly.

He chattered at her again.

Carissa just shook her head. She couldn't understand him, and until she found a voice to borrow, she couldn't explain to him how to get back to human.

Michael settled himself down next to her

with his head on her thigh.

They were both stuck.

A knock on the door sent Michael skittering across Carissa's bed and into her pillows. So the man *did* have some sense of self-preservation. Carissa smiled as she went to unlock her door.

"Oh, Carissa!" Tilly gasped as she swamped her friend in a hug that nearly knocked Carissa off her feet. "I'm so sorry!" she cried. Tears streamed down from her blue eyes.

Carissa patted her friend on the back and pulled her inside so she could shut the door again.

"I should have been there."

Carissa led her friend to the overstuffed loveseat near her table.

"I could have kept that monster from kidnapping you."

Carissa just smiled at her friend. Tilly had always been so overdramatic about things. Carissa could just imagine what was going to happen when Tilly found out that 'that monster' was hiding in her pillows.

Tilly grabbed Carissa's hands, pulling her away from her thought. "You must tell me everything!" Tilly pulled her down to sit on the seat next to her and pressed her lips to Carissa's, giving up her voice.

"Oh, Tilly," Carissa sighed as she pulled back. "You are not responsible for what happened."

Tilly looked indignant.

Carissa laughed at her. "Very well." She smiled. "It's *all* your fault, and I shall never speak to you again. That includes telling you about my marvelous misadventures."

Tilly gasped at this and bounced in her seat, making Carissa laugh.

"Okay, you're forgiven," she teased. "All right." Carissa stood up and pulled Michael's jacket off. She took it over and dropped it on the bed. "I'll tell you what happened, but you can't tell anyone about it." She looked back to her friend's widened eyes. "You have to swear."

Tilly thought about it for a moment.

Oh crap. There could be a whole lot of trouble real soon if she didn't go along with this. "I guarantee it will be worth it."

Slowly, Tilly nodded her head.

Fantastic! Carissa and Tilly had been keeping each other's secrets for a long time now. If anyone could help her with this issue, it was Tilly.

Carissa turned to the bed and looked up at the pile of pillows. Michael had buried himself well, except for the end of his tail sticking out of the middle of the pile. Oh, she was going to have to make him aware of his bits. They were going to get him in trouble one of these days.

Leaning over the edge of the bed, Carissa grabbed up the fringy end. "Your tail's hanging out."

Michael snatched it out of her hand and pulled it into the pile.

She heard Tilly get up from the loveseat and come over to look at the bed.

A low growl sounded from the pillows. He was probably upset she had betrayed his hiding place to someone.

Tilly gave Carissa a concerned look.

Carissa patted the bed. "Come on out."

The growl sounded again.

Tilly covered her mouth in shock. Mischief gleamed in her eyes. Oh yes, she knew something was up.

Carissa stood up and glared at the pile of pillows. "Either you come out, or I'll call my brother and have him deal with you."

A loud sigh sounded from the cushions, and Michael slinked his way out onto the bed.

The gasp Tilly let out upon seeing the little, white dragon was audible even without her voice.

"Tilly," Carissa held her hand out to the unhappy dragon. "I'd like you to meet Michael Duncan. Michael, this is Matilda Davenshire."

Backpedaling from the bed, Tilly tripped on the rug and landed hard on her backside. Her mouth ran frantically as she scooted across the room towards the door. Had she had a voice, she would have been hysterical.

Carissa fell on her friend, grabbing her by the arm. "You promised," she reminded Tilly.

Tilly paused and looked back up to the little dragon watching her from the bed. She nodded her head, letting Carissa know she would keep her promise.

"Michael." Carissa released her friend and turned back to the small dragon. "I think it's high time we had a proper talk."

Michael nodded his agreement and chattered at her.

"I think we should get you back to human form, first."

God, that hurt. Michael curled on his side, waiting for the rest of the pain to subside. If it hurt this much to change from one form to another, why did dragons do it? Slowly, the ache of having his bits rearrange subsided, and he sat up. It had taken Carissa twenty minutes to talk him through shifting back to human form. It felt weird to be back in his own skin. The world looked and sounded different, too. Maybe he had just gotten used to the way it looked as a dragon. Carefully, he shifted so he was sitting on the edge of the bed.

Michael rubbed his eyes and looked at the two women watching him. Carissa looked just as good now as she had the first time he saw her. Desire shot through him, pushing blood south. *Oh God, he was naked!* Grabbing one of the pillows he had been hiding in, he shoved it in his lap, hoping the two women hadn't noticed the change in his body. He looked at them. Carissa was studying his jacket just to his left, and the taller brunette Carissa had introduced as Matilda had a slight blush to her cheeks and was looking up towards the corner to his right.

Great; they had seen his reaction. So much for dignity. "So." Michael cleared his throat, trying to break the tension filling the room.

"Yes." Carissa turned away from him, heading towards what looked to be a bathroom. "Can I get you anything? Water? A towel?" She glanced back at the throw pillow he had pulled over his lap.

"Answers," he threw out.

Carissa stopped and looked at him. "Yes," she turned away again, "I suppose we all want those." She disappeared into the bathroom.

For a long moment, he sat in silence as Tilly studied him. He felt like a bug under a glass. "Hi." He smiled at her.

She gave him a mischievous smile back.

Oh, goodie!

"I'm sorry." Carissa came back out. She had stripped out of the rumpled ball gown and pulled on a black-silk robe. Without really looking at Michael, she held a large towel out towards him.

He grabbed her wrist before she could drop the towel and pull away again. "Carissa." Some reptilian part of his brain screamed *Mine!* as little bolts of electricity tingled up his arm from where he touched her, inflaming his issues to proportions that the little throw pillow was having trouble concealing. Maybe it was just those dragon pheromones still working on his brain. But—he had turned into a dragon, so they shouldn't be messing with his head anymore. Or should they be working harder on him? And how, exactly, had he become a dragon?

Shaking away the questions bouncing around in his head, he caught her eyes with his. "I didn't do it." His words were soft, but he tried to make her understand. If he could just convince her to hear him out, he could explain part of what Daniel has said. He would need to get the dossier he had put together for the rest.

Carissa studied his eyes for a moment before nodding her head.

At least she would listen to him. Michael released her hand, and she dropped the towel into his lap. He quickly swapped the towel for the inadequately small pillow. Now that his ass wasn't literally hanging out anymore, he might be able to cover it figuratively.

"It's true that I volunteered to investigate the missing people," Michael explained as he jumped up from the bed. He tucked the towel tightly around his waist and followed Carissa over to a walk-in closet as he talked. "And I did make trips to see several of the dragons that have gone missing, but it was part of my job. There's a group of us that run the solitary dragons list regularly. We keep them up to date on world activities, so they don't withdraw completely." It was dangerous to let those lone dragons go. They could easily lose touch with reality and go out rampaging.

"I did go back for coffee. Jareth asked me to…" Michael's mind caught on a fact he hadn't seen before. "Jareth." He repeated the name, turning over what he had heard and what he could remember of his file. No, it couldn't be. Tucking that though away, he saved it for later inspection. He needed more data. "Jareth asked me to bring him back a cup of coffee, but I ran into the men our investigation was pointing towards. I don't exactly remember what happened, but I ended up chained in that dungeon. I had nothing to do with your abduction. I swear."

Carissa shoved clothing around in her closet, looking for something to wear. "So how did you end up on video carrying me out of Baron Estivis' ball?"

Michael ran his hand through his hair and leaned back against the doorjamb, thinking. He thunked his head against the solid wood, trying to come up with an answer. "I don't know," he finally admitted. Nothing that came to mind sounded plausible. "I could venture a thousand guesses, but without seeing the tape, that's all they would be. Guesses."

Carissa studied him for a minute. "You had nothing to do with it?" She walked over and stood unbearably close to him.

Michael squeezed his hand into the knot on his towel in an effort not to reach out to touch her. "I swear," he said solemnly.

Carissa drew in a deep breath and studied him carefully. Slowly, she let the air out and stepped back from him. "I believe you." She nodded and turned back to her clothing. "The question now is how to get my brother and Daniel to believe you." Her fingers brushed over the hangers absently as she thought.

Michael pulled his eyes away from her and

looked up at the ceiling. "I might have an answer to that." He tipped his head over to look at her.

Carissa gave him an intrigued look.

"My mission file should have enough evidence in it to prove I didn't do it."

"But Jareth already turned in the file," Carissa pointed out. Daniel had said as much.

Michael shook his head. "True." He sighed. "But, it sounds like part of the file was missing. Yes, it showed all the information Daniel claimed, but I also had mission assignments and expense reports from those suspicious trips—proof that I had a reason to be there. If those pieces were missing, what else was left out?"

Michael ran his hand through his hair again. "It's going to be convincing them that I didn't kidnap you that will be the most trouble. If I could just get a look at that tape…" Michael let out a defeated sigh. *Shit!* Carissa's hand on his shoulder drew Michael from his study of the ceiling. God, her touch felt good on his skin.

"Let's get your file, first; then we'll worry about convincing Daniel."

The warmth in Carissa's amber eyes melted his resolve, and he swung his arms around to pull her against him. Praise all that was holy, she believed him! His lips met hers with a passion he couldn't control. That corner of his mind that screamed *Mine!* pushed him to claim her properly. Michael slid his hand down to her backside and pulled her up against him as he explored every inch of her mouth. So perfect.

Michael tugged at the belt holding the dark silk closed. Was she wearing anything under that thing? He hoped not. It would make dropping his towel and pulling her onto him so much simpler. He could already smell her arousal. She would be hot and ready for him. If he just tugged here…

A sharp, annoying noise cut into Michael's train of thought. A cough? Tilly! He pulled back from Carissa's lips as if he'd been stung, but he couldn't make his body let her go. He took two deep breaths, trying to regain his control. Oh, she was so soft, and warm, and fit him in all the right places. He took another deep breath and shut his eyes. He pulled his hands away from her and stepped back.

"Bathroom." Michael turned and beat a hasty retreat to Carissa's en suite bathroom. He had to put something solid between himself and Carissa before he physically tossed Tilly out of Carissa's room and took advantage of every flat surface he could find.

Ignoring everything else in the room, Michael made a beeline for the large, glass stall in the corner and turned the water on, full blast, as cold as he could get it. Maybe if he got it cold enough, that reptilian part of his mind screaming *Mine!* would shut up for a bit. Then again, probably not.

Chapter Ten

THE FLOOR ROSE UP TO MEET CARISSA'S BUTT AS HER knees buckled under her. *Wow!* was the only thought that flickered through her short-circuited brain. She had been kissed before, but it never tingled like that! It wouldn't be surprising if she were leaving puddles on the floor. That would be fun to explain to the maid.

Carissa looked up to find Tilly standing in the doorway, fanning herself with her hand as she stared across the bedroom to the closed bathroom door. Michael had definitely made a lasting impression on her.

Slowly coming to her senses, Tilly turned back and reached her hand down to help Carissa to her feet.

Carissa wasn't surprised when Tilly leaned in to retrieve her voice; her best friend would definitely have some choice words to say right about now.

"Ooh, Carissa Elise Markel, what have you

done?" Tilly looked back at the bathroom. The sound of running water announced the shower Michael was enjoying.

Oh, just the thought of him naked and wet made Carissa's knees weaken again. She had gotten a stellar view of him before he recalled his lack of clothing and snatched up something to hide under. She had a new favorite pillow now! Carissa shook that thought away and concentrated on Tilly. Her best friend was still looking at the bathroom door as if she wanted to break it down and join the man in the shower.

A pang of green shot through Carissa, startling her. Was she jealous of her best friend? She shook the thought away and reached out to touch Tilly, pulling her thoughts away from the bathroom. Now it was time to play swap the voice. This would be so much easier if she had thought to borrow Michael's before he'd dashed off.

"I told you they were marvelous misadventures," Carissa said as she took Tilly's voice again and turned back to her clothing. At least one of them should be dressed by the time he came back out, and since Michael would be stuck wrapped in a towel… Carissa liked the idea of him traipsing around her room in just a towel, or less. She shook her head, getting back to her story, and told Tilly about their harrowing escape as she dressed.

"You turned him into a dragon?" Tilly gasped as soon as she could. She looked back at the shut door again.

Carissa had noticed Tilly kept doing that every time Michael was mentioned. Sure, he was nice, with those sculpted muscles and light dusting of fine hair. She tingled just thinking about the way he had pulled her against him. Okay, so he was more than just nice—he was panty-drenching hot! But that didn't mean she wanted her friend thinking about him all wet and steamy in the shower…

Tilly's voice cut into Carissa's drool-worthy moment. "Do you understand what you've done?"

Seeing that Carissa had completely missed it, Tilly repeated her question.

Carissa just stared at her.

"You know the history of dragons."

Sure, Carissa nodded at her. Everyone knew the mythical beginnings of dragons.

"A king prayed to the gods to give him the power to protect his people," Tilly recited. "They gave him the power to turn into a golden dragon."

Carissa nodded. The old story was where she'd gotten the idea to make Michael a dragon.

Tilly ignored her and went on. "The king shared his power with four of his most loyal knights, creating four more colors: black, red, green, and blue."

Yes, this was well-known lore. Carissa glared at Tilly, hoping she would get to the point soon.

Tilly came to her point. "Carissa, there are no white dragons. How can Michael be white, if there are no white dragons?"

Carissa wanted to point out that his scales weren't exactly white. They were iridescent like all dragon scales, but they lacked pigment, making them translucent. They only looked white from a distance. But, that didn't matter. There were no translucent dragons, either. Carissa just shrugged instead.

"And, not to beat the subject to death, but you *made* him a *dragon!*" Tilly punctuated her words by tapping her nail on the arm of the loveseat they had settled on. "People have been trying to change others into dragons for centuries with no success, and you just thought, 'Oh, I need a dragon,' and *bam*, he's a dragon? And white! Was his hair always white?" Tilly looked back over to the closed door. Michael had been in there a long time.

"No." Carissa borrowed Tilly's voice again. "That's new." She had been rather shocked to see the change in his hair when he'd regained his human form. The lovely, chocolate-brown hair was so white it was nearly silver. A stolen glance south of his navel had proven that it wasn't just the hair on his head that had changed. That was going to be a shocker for him. Carissa glanced over to the bathroom door. Maybe she should check on him to make sure he hadn't passed out or something.

Tilly waved to get Carissa's attention again.

"I don't know how I turned him into a dragon," Carissa finally admitted with a sigh, answering Tilly's unasked question. "I just knew that we needed to get out of there, and he wasn't going to be of any help."

Tilly made kissing noises and shook her head.

"I know. I should never have gotten my mouth near his, but hindsight's twenty-twenty. We've all made stupid mistakes. This one just happens to take the cake." Carissa hung her head and sighed again. "We just have to get through it." She closed her eyes and asked herself, *But, how?*

The marble countertop was the only thing keeping Michael from falling over as he stared at his reflection in the mirror. Silvery hair and crystal-blue eyes stared back at him. He reached up to stretch out a lock so his eyes could see it directly. Yup, so white it was almost silver. Even his grandmother didn't have hair quite that color. Dropping his towel away, he checked out the rest of him to see if there were any other changes. All of his hair had gone silvery white. *Great…* At least he didn't have scales or a tail anymore. That reptilian part of his brain piped up that it liked its tail and scales.

"No you don't," Michael said sternly to his reflection. That was just going to win him awards for sanity, arguing with a bit of his brain that wanted to think for itself. That bit had given him all sorts of splendid ideas as he froze himself in the shower. Most of them consisted of parts of his anatomy and ways he could use them on Carissa. Even the frigid water hadn't done much for his state of arousal.

The shock of white hair had caught his attention in the mirror, but it was the crystal-blue eyes that drew him in. He had always had rich, chocolate-brown eyes. He liked his eyes. How could they have changed? Hell, how had he shifted into a dragon?

That little bit of brain snickered at him. *Mine!* did it.

"And how do you know that?" he growled at his reflection. Yup, definitely going for a psych eval as soon as he cleared his name.

That reptilian part uncurled a little, and memories flooded his mind. The feel of Carissa's mouth feeding him water in the dungeon. The heat boiling in him as she pressed him into the wall.

Oh God, she *had* done something to him. The question was—could it be undone?

Michael grabbed up his towel and twisted it around his waist again. He needed answers. She'd gotten hers, now it was high time Carissa gave *him* a few.

Storming through the door, Michael looked around the room. Carissa and Tilly were perched on a loveseat in the little sitting area. Dropping himself into one of the overstuffed armchairs next to them, he studied the two women. They had fallen silent when he'd come out. Taking a deep breath, Michael turned his attention to Carissa. God, she looked lovely in that fitted T-shirt and jeans. *Mine!* He shook the thought away and focused. "I just have one question." Michael pinned Carissa with his eyes. "How did I turn into a dragon?" Then, a better question hit him. "No, better yet, can you fix whatever you did?" He could tell the answer by the sorrow that crept into her eyes.

"No." Carissa shook her head. "It can't be undone."

The finality of her words made that reptilian part of his brain wiggle about happily. "Great. So I'm stuck with this peanut gallery in my head," Michael huffed, shaking his head to silence his wayward bit.

"Peanut gallery?" Carissa asked, sounding worried.

"I've got this *voice*," Michael tapped an area just behind his right ear, "tucked away in the back of my head that keeps giving me running commentary on everything."

Carissa exchanged worried looks with Tilly.

Great, now they thought he was crazy. Could this day get any better?

Having come to some silent agreement, Carissa turned back to him. "If I had to venture a guess, I would say it was your brain's way of dealing with the instincts you've gained."

Tilly nodded her agreement with Carissa's words.

"Either that, or I've gone schizophrenic," Michael snarked.

"Maybe a little." Carissa chuckled at his jest. "But, I would listen when that voice spoke."

"If I'd listened to that voice, I wouldn't have had to run out all of your cold water." Michael glared at her. "And we wouldn't be sitting here talking. Moaning, maybe, but definitely not talking." His blood pooled below his towel just thinking about some of the suggestions his brain had given him.

Color rushed up Carissa's face as she caught on to his less-than-proper meaning.

"Sorry," he grumbled, looking away from her. *Damn it!* He fidgeted in his chair, trying to get his mind away from the feel of her skin against his. He wasn't some dumb teenager with his first dirty magazine.

"It's all right." Carissa sighed. "You're brooding."

This shocked Michael into looking at her. "*What?*" he snapped.

"You're brooding," she answered calmly.

"No. No. *No.* Kids brood. Teenagers brood. Adults do not *brood*," Michael denied.

Tilly actually laughed at him, earning her a glare.

"Adults *do* brood," Carissa explained. "Usually, males only brood when around females during their fertile periods, but your hormone levels are all over the place."

"Great." Michael threw up his hands and tilted his head back to stare at the ceiling. "Why don't you just call the king and have him lock me up now?" It would be safer that way. A dragon wacked out on hormones could be a danger to himself and every female in a hundred miles. He had seen the kinds of damage an out-of-control dragon could cause.

"I don't see a need for that," Carissa soothed him. "You're system is probably just overproducing due to stress. Give it a few days, and it should settle out."

"I don't have a few days," Michael pointed out. "The longer I take to come forwards, the harder it's going to be to prove my innocence."

"Then we had best get started." Carissa changed the subject. "How do you plan on proving your innocence?"

Now this was a topic Michael felt he could handle. He sat up straighter in his chair as he spoke. "Something about the information I'd been collecting didn't sit well with me, so I mailed out a copy to go over with a friend later. I figured a fresh set of eyes on the problem might solve it easier." Michael was now glad he had thought of that.

"So, all we have to do is get out of here, find this file, and take it to Daniel." Carissa nodded as she thought about the plan.

"There is no 'we' here," Michael pointed out. "I need to get the file and take it to Daniel. There's no reason for you to get more involved." He finally agreed with that reptilian part of his brain. He was not going to put her in possible danger again.

"Let me remind you of your situation." Carissa pinned him with a stern look, crossing her arms just under her chest. "You're a full-grown dragon who doesn't know the first thing about being a dragon, in the middle of a brooding."

She might have a point there.

"Think wild mood swings, uncontrollable urges, and top it off with not knowing how to switch between forms."

Okay, that one hit it on the head.

"You need help."

Michael stared at her, wanting to deny this fact. He had worked hard to earn his place in Eternity, and it hurt his pride to admit that he needed help—especially from someone with such perfect breasts. Did she have to push them up like that? It made it hard for him to think. "All right," Michael caved. "You have a valid point." He had also learned to admit to his limits before they got him killed. "Any ideas?"

Carissa grinned at him. "Maybe."

Oh, crap. What had he just started?

Chapter Eleven

"This isn't working."

Carissa pinched the bridge of her nose as Michael sat up from the bed, complaining. He had been trying for ten minutes to shift back to dragon form. "It will." She sat on the edge of the bed and pressed him to lie back down. "Just close your eyes and relax." She stroked her fingers over the taut muscles of his chest.

Letting out an exasperated sigh, Michael closed his eyes and tried again. "I can't." He gritted his teeth a few moments later. "No matter how hard I try, I just can't do it."

His muscles had tensed even further under Carissa's fingers.

"I just don't understand how you can stand it. It hurts too damn much."

Aha! There lies the problem.

"Sit up," Carissa urged as she scooted closer to him, tucking her feet under her.

Michael gave her a considering look before sitting up.

Carissa held out her arms. "Come here."

Michael stared at her, unmoving.

"Just trust me."

Letting out the breath he was holding, Michael leaned in so she could pull him into her arms.

Carissa sighed as he wrapped his arms around her. Man, he felt good. "Relax." She tucked his head in so it rested on her shoulder with his face buried in the side of her neck. Rubbing circles into his back, she tried to soothe his rigid posture. Slowly, he drew in a deep breath and started to relax into her arms. Finally!

"Shifting only hurts if you force it." Carissa rocked slightly as she spoke. She leaned her head over on top of his. "Just relax and let it happen." She held him for a moment, trying to think of something else she could do to help him understand how to let go. *Of course!* She nearly laughed as it hit her. "Just ask your peanut gallery."

Michael tensed for a moment before nodding and relaxing against her again.

Magic tingled against Carissa's skin as Michael's form shifted, leaving the little dragon clinging to her shoulder. "See, that wasn't so bad." Carissa kissed him on top of the head before lifting him off and setting him on the bed next to her. Maybe now he wouldn't have so much of an issue shifting again.

Michael chattered at her unintelligently.

Smiling, she petted down his back and turned her attention to where Tilly was waiting. "Thank you. Just get us outside." Carissa stood to give her friend back her voice, but Tilly waved her away.

She mouthed something that made Carissa smile.

"You're right. I might need it," she replied, accepting the use of Tilly's voice. The magic letting Carissa borrow it wouldn't last much longer, but it might come in handy.

Sitting on the edge of the bed, Carissa shifted without bothering to undress. She wiggled out of her clothing and stretched her wings. Oh, it felt good to be back in this form. Ignoring the basket Tilly placed on the bed, Carissa turned her attention to Michael. She had thought he was cute, but he looked so much better with her dragon vision.

All dragons shimmered, but Michael's translucent scales cut the light in a way she had never seen before. With human eyes, he looked white. With the enhanced vision of dragons, he sparkled with rainbow hues. Once the world figured out who he was, there was no way he would ever be able to hide among dragons. It didn't help that he had taken the shape of the golden dragons. None of the other colors had the frill, horns, and tufty tail. Other than the lack of color, he could have been her brother's twin. She was so going to be in trouble when this got out. Or, maybe, if she found a way to glamor him to gold, he would make a decent body double for the king. *Hmm… That's worth thinking about.*

Shaking away future possibilities, Carissa turned her mind to what they had to do now. They needed to get moving. From the way Michael was watching her, she was sure his mind was somewhere else entirely. Time to snap him back to reality. Carissa closed the distance between them and rubbed her shoulder up his side with enough pressure to push him back as she passed.

He staggered sideways before shaking his head and following her to the basket Tilly held.

A quick snap of wings got Carissa to the edge of the basket, and she dropped down into the laundry.

It took Michael a little longer to jump up and in. He circled Carissa before settling down with his tail curled around her protectively.

It was a very dominant move, one Carissa had seen males make with their mates or young. It staked a claim to her that she didn't feel he had a right to make. Chattering at him, she shoved him away with her front paw, making him unwrap his tail.

Michael chattered back angrily as he righted himself, but he settled with his tail wrapped up his other side.

Carissa looked up as Tilly peeked over the edge of the basket at them. The light in her eyes told Carissa that her friend had some choice comments to make about them. Suddenly, she was glad she had Tilly's voice. "The roof," Carissa chattered in dragon.

Tilly nodded her understanding and dropped the wrinkled ball gown on top of them.

Carissa leaned in against Michael's warmth and closed her eyes to relax. It would take Tilly a little while to sneak them out so they could make their escape. Might as well enjoy the ride.

Michael felt a rumble of pleasure issue from his chest as Carissa leaned into his side. That reptilian part of his brain screamed *Mine!* as he leaned his head over onto hers. It was next to impossible to ignore that voice while he was in this form. He had this near-insatiable urge to wrap his tail back around her, but Carissa had made it clear she didn't want that. Why, he wasn't exactly sure.

Protect Mine!, the voice pressed at Michael.

I will, Michael tried to press back. The memory of her missing scale ate at him. He had left her vulnerable. That sat with him about as well as a splinter under a fingernail. His tail thrashed, wanting to make its way back around her. 'No!' he told it and chomped down on the ends of his tuft. He mouthed the fringe gently before picking one strand and chewing on it lightly. It was somewhat soothing. A snicker from Carissa drew his attention. Amusement gleamed in her amber eyes.

"Only children suckle on their tails," she chirped, reaching out to draw the strand from his mouth.

Michael stared at her. He had understood her! He chirped back at her, but it only sounded like high squeaking. He felt her chuckle at him.

"Just relax and let your instincts lead."

Michael nodded and let the voice he had been fighting tell him what to do. "*Mine!*" he rumbled unintelligently as his tail wrapped itself back around Carissa again. He shuddered at the strength with which his instincts pulled at him. The tufty end of Carissa's tail whapped into the side of his head, rocking his brain back into focus.

"I said let them lead, not give in to them," she growled at him.

"Sorry," he chirped. This time it sounded like

a word to him. He pulled his tail back so it wasn't pressed into her, but that was as far as he could force himself to back off. Something in him had claimed her, and it was damned hard to control that bit.

"It's okay," Carissa rumbled. "You're still brooding."

Michael opened his mouth to deny it, but a warning shake from Tilly shut them both up. Michael cocked his head and could hear voices outside the basket.

"Oh, Tilly."

They both froze at the sound of the king's voice.

"Have you had a chance to talk with Carissa?"

Michael tightened his tail around Carissa as he felt her tense. They waited with baited breath as Tilly made some kind of nonverbal response.

"I see," Kyle's voice sounded again. "Please keep an eye on her. I'm afraid this whole kidnapping and betrayal business has upset her more than she's letting on. I've never seen her run off like that before. I promise you this Michael Duncan will spend a long time paying for what he's done to her."

Sharp teeth came down on Michael's tail, startling him out of the angry growl that had started in his chest. He turned shocked eyes to where Carissa was spitting out his tufts. Her eyes held a warning to be quiet. They both turned their attention back as the king finished talking.

"All right, but please let me know if there is anything I can do. I'm worried about her."

Tilly made some response that made Kyle laugh.

"Thank you. I know she will."

With that comment, the basket started swaying as Tilly started on her way again. Close call.

Michael sighed to himself as they both relaxed in silence.

A few more minutes of swaying and empty halls saw Tilly setting the basket down and drawing out the dress.

Michael blinked in the bright light of the afternoon sun.

"Come on," Carissa chirped and jumped out of the basket.

Michael followed her over the side and onto the ledge surrounding the top of the building. Michael was familiar with this building—it was the king's main residence when he was in the city. It was only a few blocks down from Eternity's main offices and a few miles from his own townhouse. He looked over the edge of the ten-story building to the streets below. Wow, that was a long way down.

"How are we getting down?" Michael asked

as he paced along the edge. There had to be a fire escape somewhere around here that would lead them to the ground. The rustle of wings drew Michael's attention back as Carissa threw herself off the building and caught the updraft.

"Oh no!" Michael backed up from the edge. He may have wings, but he did not know the first thing about flying. And jumping off a ten-story building was not his idea of a test flight.

"Come on," Carissa called as she circled around him. "Just spread you wings. It's easy." She flapped a few times, showing him how.

Michael jumped down and ran away from the edge. "Maybe for *you*."

"Wimp!" she cried.

"Better a wimp than a *splat* on the ground," he growled and raced away from her.

Laughing, she dive-bombed him.

He turned away from her attack. What was that crazy woman trying to do?

She buzzed him a few more times. Her last dive landed her square on his back.

He screamed out as her claws nabbed onto his wings and she hurled him into the air... right over the side of the building.

Flipping several times in the air, his wings finally popped open about halfway down as his instincts kicked in. Michael beat them for all he was worth and was delighted when his flight leveled out.

Carissa wheeled in next to him, laughing.

"What the hell!" he growled at her.

Carissa laughed again. "Dragons are born with the instincts to fly," she cooed, wheeling around him.

"I wasn't born a dragon," Michael snapped.

"Maybe not, but you still have instincts," she pointed out before closing her wings and dropping out of the sky.

Michael's heart dropped just as fast, and he closed his wings to chase her. He couldn't let her hit the ground!

Carissa's wings snapped open just feet from the concrete.

Michael followed suit and glided up behind her. As his fear subsided, joy slowly took over. Beating his wings, he overtook Carissa. He pulled a few fast corners and loops, testing out his new ability. This was fun!

"So, where are we going?" she asked as she pulled up even with him.

His mind came back from the joys of flight to what they had to do. "My place." Michael turned and angled towards his home.

Chapter Twelve

THE THREE-STORY TOWNHOUSE WAS LOVELY. CARISSA considered the quiet home from where they perched across the street. Why Michael hadn't just flown up to his house had confused her, but watching it now, there was definitely something that bothered her about it, too.

Michael's head swung back and forth as he scanned his road. "Come on." He turned away from the house.

Carissa looked at it for a moment longer before following her companion across his neighbor's roof and down over the backyard.

Flying low over the ground, he dodged between trees and toys until he was several houses down.

Carissa glanced back the way they had come. It would have been so much easier just to cross the street. Holding her tongue, she followed him across the street between two cars. She had to flap hard to make it through before the second one hit her. What the hell was he thinking?

With a loud crunch of breaking branches, Michael crashed into a bush on his side of the street.

Following him in, Carissa pulled up short as he paused, looking around. "What are you *doing*?" she hissed at him.

He just shook his head and tucked his wings in. Scurrying along the fence line, Michael took off towards the back of the yard.

Carissa let out an exasperated sigh and followed. They crawled under bushes and squeezed through fences until they reached the back of the blue house Michael had claimed was his.

Crouching as low as he could, Michael scanned the backyard before shooting across the open grass to a small flap in the back door.

Carissa chased after him.

A couple of good knocks with his shoulder popped the old cat flap open, and he squeezed inside.

Carissa tucked in her wings and followed the end of his tufty tail. The sight that met her stopped her in her tracks. What had once been a well-maintained kitchen was now in shambles. The drawers were pulled out, and junk was dumped everywhere.

Michael slinked his way through the mess and stopped just inside the door, listening.

Carissa followed him carefully. Now she

128

understood why he had been so cautious about approaching his home.

Michael took off down the hall, leaving Carissa standing in the doorway. She stared into his living room, shocked by the sight of it.

The kitchen had been bad, but the living room was worse. Someone had taken a blade to just about everything the man owned. Cushion foam was torn up and tossed everywhere. Books had been massacred. Even the painting above the mantel had been shredded. Either Michael had had a major fit before he left, or someone had been looking for something.

"All's clear," Michael said as he came back down the hall, pulling the belt of his bathrobe tight.

Apparently, he wasn't having an issue shifting between forms any more.

He dropped a second terrycloth robe over Carissa as he turned back down the hallway.

Taking the hint, Carissa shifted and pulled the large robe on before chasing after him. The rest of his house was just as bad as the living room. "What happened?" Carissa asked as she looked over the shredded mattress that had been on his bed.

Michael bent into the closet and started pulling out what had been clean clothing. "Eternity." He sighed. "They probably came in looking for some clue as to where I was." He wrinkled his nose at the claw marks rending the front of his shirt before tossing it towards an overturned wastebasket. "Although, I've never known them to get this destructive. They must have been really upset."

Carissa's eyes finally identified the cause of the destruction. She had assumed the cuts were from a knife, but closer inspection showed multiple jagged lines. Someone had shifted to dragon form and torn through his place.

Michael picked up another shirt—this one was whole—and handed it to her.

"And you're okay with this?" Carissa asked as she rubbed the shirt between her fingers.

"No. I'm not okay with it," Michael growled, and then he let out a sigh. "But, I understand it. If they thought I was killing dragons..." He let the subject drop as he went back to searching for clothing.

"How are we going to find your file in this mess?" Carissa pulled off the bathrobe and slipped into Michael's shirt. It hung low enough that it was almost decent.

"We're not." Michael handed her a pair of jeans. There was a tear down the front of the leg, but it looked more artful than damaged.

A belt followed, and she pulled on the oversized pants and secured them in place.

"The file was never here." Michael found

another set of clothing that wasn't too bad off and quickly changed into them. "I mailed it to a friend of mine."

Carissa looked around at the mess. "Then what are we doing here?" She was sure his home had been lovely before someone had ransacked it.

"Getting dressed." Michael found two socks and pulled them on. "I'm not sure what Terrance would do if we showed up at his house as dragons." He shrugged as he fished a boot out from under what was left of his bed. "He's a bit of a nutcase."

Carissa gave him a pointed look. "And you thought to send him a file on dragon disappearances?" she questioned.

Michael shrugged again and collected the second boot from behind a desk. This one looked slightly chewed. "He might believe in the second shooter on the grassy knoll, but he's one of the best statisticians I've ever met." Michael struggled into the boots before standing up and scanning the room again. "Anyway, I've known him for a long time. If Eternity's put a price on my head, then he's the one person I can trust to not turn me in."

Looking at the mess they'd left, Carissa was sure that Eternity had put a bounty out for Michael.

"Here." Michael handed her a pair of leather moccasins tied together. They'd been hanging over what was left of the ceiling fan.

Taking them, Carissa worked the leather thongs apart and pulled them on. "How are we going to get there?" she asked as she stood up in the oversized shoes.

Michael held out a ratty-looking, leather jacket. "In style." He smiled and led the way out.

Thank goodness he hadn't told his boss about the arrangement he had with his neighbor. Michael smiled as he opened up the gate in his side fence and let Carissa into the little shed in Mrs. Giuffria's backyard. Thin light filtered in through the dirty window, shining over a multitude of gardening supplies. The grandmotherly woman had donated a small section of her storage area in payment for his help tilling her garden in the springtime. Two days of backbreaking work was turning out to be well worth it.

"We're going on *that?*" Carissa gasped as he pulled back the brown tarp covering a Harley Roadster. He had spent a long time fixing the old bike up.

"Yup." Pulling a tight-fitting riding jacket out of a locker, he slipped it on over his shirt. "Fastest thing I have." He handed her a helmet before pulling another out. "Besides, the full-face shields will help hide our identities from the guys watching the house."

Carissa stared at him stunned. "What?"

"You didn't see the van sitting just down the street?" Michael set his helmet on the bike and took hers. Carefully, he gathered up her hair. He loved how it tangled around his fingers. She was so warm under his hands. All he had to do was... He pushed away the voice egging him on and tucked the golden curls up on her head so he could put her helmet on her. Now was not the time for what he wanted to do. "They probably had someone watching my back fence, too, but they might not expect us to come out of my neighbor's yard. It should give us time to get away." Turning from Carissa, Michael popped his helmet on and opened up the door.

Rolling the bike out onto the concrete pad, Michael shut the shed up before climbing on the bike.

"Wait." Carissa grabbed his arm before he could start the thing up. "I've never been on one of these."

"And I've never flown," Michael teased through his open face shield. "Now climb on." He nodded to the seat behind him. "At least I don't have to toss you off a ten-story building for this." He smiled at her.

Carissa considered him for a moment before shutting her helmet and climbing up on the seat behind him.

"Just hold on." Michael tucked Carissa's arms around his middle. "Everything will be fine."

Flicking his helmet closed, Michael fired up the old Harley. God, it felt good to be back on his bike. This was a thrill he knew. Kicking it into gear, he took off, making Carissa grab onto him tighter. A rumble of pleasure shivered up from his chest. Even through his protective gear, she felt wonderful.

Michael shook his head slightly and forced his concentration back to the bike and the road ahead of him. A flash in his mirror drew his attention just in time to see a dark SUV pull out to follow them. Reaching down, Michael tightened Carissa's hold on him before twisting the accelerator and dropping the bike down a gear. The SUV kicked it up, too, and raced after Michael as he shot out into traffic.

So, someone did know about his bike. Well, he knew a few tricks they didn't.

Slipping in and out of traffic, Michael tried to lose his tail, but the driver stuck to him. Whoever was driving that thing was damn good. Michael cut a hard right, making Carissa squeeze him tighter. Damn, he was going to have to take her riding sometime when he could really enjoy the feel of her pressing into his back. Putting that thought out of his mind, he pulled a hard left into the local park.

He could hear Carissa squeal as he hopped the curb and pointed his bike into a gap in the trees. His little Roadster wasn't really made for trail riding, but that SUV sure wouldn't be able to follow him.

A few minutes of bumpy, dirt trails spilled them out on the other side of the park, free of Eternity's radar. For now. Michael could feel Carissa's angry rumbles against his back. Surely she couldn't fault his choice of escape routes. Okay, so it hadn't been the smoothest ride, but it had gotten the job done. He concentrated on keeping the bike between the ditches as the image of her anger-filled eyes floated in the back of his mind. God, she was beautiful when she was angry. With those luscious curls all rumpled up from being under that helmet. That ever-present voice joined in with his imagination, tightening his pants to an uncomfortable point. Man, when he got out of this, he was going to have to find himself a nice girlfriend. His peanut gallery cried out for the woman behind him. That would be great, but he truly doubted she would have him. She was, after all, the king's sister.

Thirteen

FULL NIGHT HAD FALLEN BY THE TIME MICHAEL TUCKED his bike in between a rusting-out pickup and a worn farmhouse and shut it down.

Carissa wasn't sure how she felt about her first ride on a motorcycle. The first part had been a bit hair-raising, and she definitely hadn't liked the shortcut through the woods, but Michael had handled both of those parts with expert skill. Her jangled nerves had finally settled after they lost Eternity and Michael sent the bike tooling down the open road. That part had been amazing. She had even relaxed into the purr of the motor and Michael's warm back. His rich spice and the hint of dragon musk had lulled her back-brain into several very nice fantasies. Maybe, when this was all over, she might find a way to entice him into trying a few of them out.

Reluctantly, Carissa pulled her hands out of the pockets on Michael's coat and got off the bike. She pulled her helmet off and looked up at the old house while Michael rummaged in the bag on the side of the bike.

Standing in the shadow of the moonlit house, Carissa couldn't really see much, but the place looked deserted. The white paint on the clapboard siding curled away, and a shutter on one of the windows hung at a precarious angle in obvious disrepair. Why had Michael brought her here? Weren't they going to see his friend and pick up some information?

"Does your friend live here?" Carissa asked as Michael finished slipping a metal plate between the kickstand of the bike and the soft earth under it.

He chuckled and set his helmet on the motorcycle. "Something like that." Taking her headgear, he perched it on the seat. "This way." Michael turned and led her down a narrow path to the back of the building.

Carissa's breath caught as Michael stepped from the shadows. The moonlight twinkled in the soft silver of his hair with the same iridescence of dragon scales. It gave him an almost ethereal look that stole her breath away. Images of moonlight playing over his toned skin danced in her head. Yummy!

"Over here."

Michael's voice cut into her thoughts, and she quickened her stalled feet to his side.

Michael bent into the tall grass and pulled up

what looked to be a door.

Carissa glanced into the gaping hole. A set of wooden stairs led down into the black abyss. It must have been some kind of storm shelter.

Michael pulled a penlight from his inner pocket and pointed it into the hole. The thin beam didn't do much to dispel the darkness. "After you." He held his hand out for her to lead the way.

You have got to be kidding! Carissa gave him a questioning look before taking the light he held. A deep breath bolstered her courage, and she stepped from the packed earth onto the first of the rickety-looking steps. Surprisingly, they were a lot sturdier than they appeared.

Descending into the dusty vault, Carissa looked around in what little light filtered in from the doorway. It was definitely a storm shelter. Boxes of supplies were stacked neatly along the walls. Her study of the room was cut short as Michael pulled the planks of wood serving as the door shut. She clutched onto the little Maglite as he made his way down to her side.

Michael pointed to the back of the room. "Over here." He knocked on a flat space between two shelves. Two heavy pounds, followed by three short raps. Wrapping an arm around her shoulders, Michael drew Carissa in against his side and waited.

Carissa studied the flat space, but she couldn't see anything remarkable about it. The pop and hiss of a speaker coming to life echoed through the room.

"How is a raven like a writing desk?" a voice boomed out from a corner behind her.

Carissa whipped her head around to look for the source of the sound, but Michael held her in place against him.

"Your hair wants for cutting," he answered.

What kind of answer was that? Carissa looked at him, confused.

"Michael?" the voice asked. There was a note of disbelief in it.

"In the flesh." Michael shot the wall a toothy grin. "Can I come in? It's cold out here, and there are wolves." The seconds ticked by as they waited for a response. A hissing noise came from the wall.

Carissa gasped in surprise as part of the brick-work swung open. A tall man with dark skin stood framed in the doorway.

"God, man, it's good to see you." The man stepped out of the doorway and took Michael's hand. He pulled Michael in for what might have passed as a hug. It was more a chest bump and slap on the back. "I didn't think I would ever see you again. Did you know that there's a BOLO out on you?"

"I kind of figured." Michael pulled away from

his friend and turned back to Carissa. He placed his hand on her back and brought her forwards into the light.

"Carissa, I would like you to meet Terrence Basha," Michael said, introducing the man. "Terrence, this is Carissa Markel. She's helping me."

Terrence looked at her with wide eyes. "Carissa Markel! As in the dragon king's *sister?*"

Michael nodded. "One and the same."

"My Lady." Terrence took her hand and kissed it.

Carissa could feel Michael's hand tense on her back. "Good evening." She smiled and pulled her hand back. It would be better if she kept her distance from Terrence. Michael was obviously still brooding. There was no telling what might set his protective instincts off.

Terrence looked from her to Michael and back.

Carissa could see that he had picked up on something in Michael's posture that set him on edge.

"Well, don't just stand there. Come in." Terrence stepped back, clearing the doorway. "I've been going over that file you sent me."

Carissa relaxed a little as Michael's hand softened against her back. She stepped over the edge of a metal doorframe. It was raised several inches from the floor with a rubber gasket wrapped around its curved edge, very like bulkhead doors on ships. The room that opened up in front of her was unique. Living room, office, kitchen, and bedroom all rolled into one long room.

"Did you find anything?" Michael asked as he followed her in.

A fallout shelter! Carissa's eyes finally recognized the utilitarian building for what it was. The man was living in a *fallout shelter!* What kind of weirdo were they dealing with?

"Lots of stuff," Terrence answered as he pulled the door shut and sealed them in. "I think you might have a bigger problem on your hands than you thought. And, what did you do to your hair?"

"It's a long story." Michael sighed and ran his hand through his white locks. "Can you show me what you've got?"

"Sure."

Carissa stood there, forgotten, as the two men made their way to a table covered in papers. Stifling a yawn, she found a comfortable-looking, oversized beanbag and helped herself to it. The last few days had been amazingly long. She listened to the men chatter on, trying to understand, but the rise and fall of their voices eased her into sleep.

"What is she to you?"

Terrence's words drew Michael's attention away from his study of Carissa's sleeping face. God, she was beautiful. Michael would love to wake up to that face every morning, with her soft curls tangled around her head and those luscious lips slightly parted. Desire burned in him again. For a while, he had been able to push her from his mind and concentrate on figuring out his puzzle, but now that he had his answers, it came back with a vengeance.

"She saved me." Michael turned back to his friend. He had already told Terrence about their escape.

Terrence looked up at Michael's white hair. "She did a bit more than just that." His change in nature had been included in the story. "And, she stuck around. What are you going to do, now?"

"What do you mean?" Michael glanced back at Carissa. He had an idea of where Terrence was going.

"Are you going to try and keep her?"

Yup, he went there. "How can I?" Michael let out a forlorn sigh. "She's the king's sister, and I...

well, I'm a security guard." When it all boiled down, that's all he was. Protection for dragons.

"One hell of a security guard," Terrence scoffed at him. "Michael, you have one of the most prestigious jobs on the planet. Very few can even make it into your position. You work long, hard hours to make sure that people like her are safe in this world. You deserve something nice."

"Even more reason to let her go. I don't have time to pursue her, even if she wasn't out of my league," Michael pointed out. His insides screamed that he was wrong, but he ignored them. He was starting to get good at ignoring them.

"And that's it," Terrence huffed. "You're just going to let her go?"

Michael looked at Carissa longingly, but nodded.

"Man, if I was in your shoes, I'd start by tagging that."

"*What?*" Michael snapped.

"Hell yeah. Look, you have a fine piece there, and she's obviously into you."

"Says the man who's ready for zombies," Michael scoffed. "When was the last time you got out of here?"

"Hey, zombies could happen," Terrence said defensively. "Anyway, I was out last Thursday."

Michael raised an eyebrow at this.

"The gun show was in town, and I needed some more powder."

"Terrence. Once-a-month tours of the local hardware supplier do not make a social life," Michael pointed out. "You need to get out of this hole. Your grandmother left you a very nice farmhouse that's falling to pieces just outside. Hell, once this thing's blown over, I'll get some of the guys together, and we'll come out and help you fix it up."

"Sure, put me out there in the open, undefended."

"Aliens are not going to come kidnap you, the government doesn't want your brain, and Bigfoot has better things to do than flounce through your flowerbeds."

"And when we were kids, dragons didn't exist."

"Touché." Michael had to concede that point.

"What are you going to do about the dragon thing?" Terrence changed the subject.

Michael ran his hand through his hair, ruffling up the white locks again. "I don't know." He sighed. "Carissa said the hormone thing should settle out in a few days."

Terrence shot him a cheesy grin.

Michael had accidently mentioned his brooding. That had been an interesting conversation. "And

I think I'm getting the hang of the rest of it." Except for that reptilian voice that was currently laughing at him. What the hell did it know that he didn't? "I'm going to have to stop in for a psych eval, but I'm sure I can handle anything unexpected."

"Yeah man, whatever." Terrence gave him a skeptical look. "The way I see it, Carissa's responsible for you being a dragon. She should be the one to teach you what you need to know."

Michael glared at him as that inner voice agreed with Terrence.

"She could at least help you with the hormone problem." Terrence snickered.

Michael sighed, trying to ignore the screams of *Mine!* in his head. "I'll think about it."

"Do that. You deserve someone nice."

Terrence did have a point there. Michael's last girlfriend had started out nice, but she had gotten rather needy fast. She told him that he was spending too much time at his job and had given him an ultimatum; so, he let her go. That went over about as well as porcupines at a petting zoo. And it didn't help when his neighbors called the cops. They took one look at his Eternity identification and hauled her to jail, leaving him to clean up the three windows she had broken. Terrence's old-fashioned clock chimed six times, drawing Michael back to the present. Hell,

145

was it that late already?

Terrence stood up and stretched. "If you plan to take this to Daniel tomorrow, you'd better get some sleep."

"True." Michael stood up and looked around the room. Terrence had one bed and that nice, cozy beanbag. Michael had spent several nights stretched out on the oversized thing, but Carissa was currently occupying it. He looked up to Terrence for an answer to his dilemma.

"The beanbag's big enough for two." Terrence chuckled before heading for his bed.

Michael looked down at it. He had slept double on futons that were half the size of that thing, but to cuddle up against Carissa... Could he do that? The voice in his head told him *definitely*. But, should he? That he wasn't sure about.

Terrence chuckled again as he clicked off the overhead light, dropping the shelter into its night-time mode.

An eerie, green glow from the small panels flooded the room with just enough light for Michael to make out shapes. Letting out a sigh, he kicked off his boots. Unless he wanted to brush the papers off the table, there really wasn't any other place to sleep.

Pulling the beanbag away from the wall, Michael lay down on the high side, pushing the filling around until the surface was nearly flat. Letting out a sigh, Carissa rolled over. Michael froze as she snuggled into his side, with her head nearly on his shoulder. Her hand came to rest on his chest. Damn, she felt good. Slowly, he drew in a breath and wrapped his arm around her. Carissa let out a contented sigh before dropping back into a deeper sleep. Maybe Terrence was right. Maybe he had a chance.

Mine! the voice screamed again.

Or maybe he was just a delusional idiot with wacked-out hormones. He adjusted his ever-present issue and closed his eyes. Matching his breathing to her steady rhythm, he tried to shut up the voice telling him to claim the luscious creature next to him. He was mostly successful, but man, were his dreams going to be carnal tonight.

Chapter Fourteen

"ARE YOU SURE ABOUT THIS?" CARISSA LOOKED AT THE little dragon next to her.

Michael nodded his head, unable to speak. The magic holding Tilly's voice had worn off during the night, so Carissa had to borrow his.

Carissa looked over the dash of Terrence's pickup truck. The thing drove amazingly well for the condition it appeared to be in.

When she woke up this morning wrapped in Michael's arms, a lot of things passed through her mind, but turning him in hadn't been one of them. Yet, here they were, sitting in the lot across the street from the main office of Eternity. Michael had woven a strong case for this course of action. It had the highest possibility of working, but it made Carissa uneasy. If just one thing went wrong, Michael would be in the hands of Eternity. And if the information he had discovered was correct, there was no way he would live to see a fair trial.

Carissa looked at the guarded gates one last time before opening her borrowed leather jacket and letting the little dragon crawl inside. When he poked his head back out, she kissed him on top of it. "For luck."

Michael purred at her and nuzzled her cheek before retreating back down inside the coat.

Carissa took a fortifying breath and tucked the thick, manila envelope inside the coat with Michael. He had explained how that one folder held everything he had collected on the missing dragons and the ring responsible for taking them. Terrence had made a copy just in case. It was amazing how paranoid one person could be.

Zipping the jacket up, Carissa got out of the car and hurried towards the building. She knew the moment the guards at the gate recognized her. There was a flurry of activity as calls were made for additional men.

"Lady Markel!" A broad man in a black uniform met her halfway across the street. He latched onto her elbow and pulled her back to the safety of the building. "Are you all right?" he asked, looking over her.

Carissa nodded her head to reassure the guard. For this plan to work, they had to think she'd freed herself, and that meant no voice.

149

"Get her inside." The broad man handed her off to two more men, who rushed her past the standard checkpoints, unmolested. Being kidnapped sure made secure places easy to get into.

Carissa clutched the neck of her jacket together as they walked down several halls. She had been in this building enough to recognize the route to medical. That was not where she needed to go.

"This way, My Lady," the guards said, trying to redirect Carissa when she made the turn she wanted.

Carissa pushed their hands away and ignored them. Unsure of whom to actually trust, Michael had made it clear that she should only talk to Daniel.

"Please, My Lady, this way." The man tried to stop her.

She ignored him and took the hall that would lead her to the main offices. When his hand gripped her elbow, restraining her, Carissa wheeled around, breaking his grip. "I'm here to see Daniel," she informed her guards before turning back to find her destination. "I know where Michael is." This got their attention.

The second man reached for her shoulder and stopped her again. "Tell us." There was a definite note of anger in his voice. Oh yes, these men would definitely hurt Michael. Were they involved, or just

150

upset that one of their number would hurt the people they were sworn to protect?

She turned away from them and tried to continue down the hall. "I will speak with Daniel."

"Then come with us to medical, and we'll get him for you," the first man pleaded.

Man, these men were pushy! A thought hit Carissa that made her smile as she ignored her escort. Her brother had probably been livid when he'd found her gone. Kyle would have definitely threatened all of them if they didn't find her unhurt. That would explain why they were so determined to get her to medical. Carissa ignored them and hurried down the hall to Daniel's office. Someone had probably called the king as soon as she had crossed the road… She had to hurry before he showed up. Now *that* was truly a scary thought!

Carissa's feet picked up speed, and she raced down the halls, trailing the bewildered guards after her. Seeing Daniel's office door open, Carissa burst into the room without knocking.

Daniel's surprised face looked up from behind his desk.

"Leave us." Carissa added a hint of magic to the order and slammed it into the men huffing behind her.

Both of them stopped dead in their tracks

and left.

A moment of silence followed as Carissa met the green eyes of Eternity's director.

He looked her over.

Michael's ratty leather jacket and oversized clothing probably made her look like some homeless kid. It didn't help that she had twisted her hair up in a loose bun that was starting to come undone. Realizing that she probably did look somewhat abused, she took as regal a posture as she could muster. That may have also explained why the guards were so adamant about getting her to medical.

Daniel rustled some papers on his desk before speaking. "Do you think it was wise to send them out with such an open order?" He looked past her to the open door.

Carissa almost laughed; of all the things he could say, he was worried about his men first. That was one of the things she loved about him. Always looking after his people. "They may wander around for a bit, but they'll be fine." Carissa relaxed. Daniel would listen to her.

Nodding his head, he accepted her words. "And how are you?" He turned his attention to her again.

"Unhurt." Carissa turned and shut Daniel's office door, locking it. This was a conversation they needed to have in private. "I'm not interrupting any-thing?" she asked, turning back to him.

He looked at the closed door and raised an eyebrow. "Nothing important." Standing up, he turned a chair around for her. "What can I do for you?" He showed Carissa into the seat and sat in an-other so they were almost facing.

Carissa took a deep breath and considered him. Daniel was shorter than Michael was. He was also broader in the shoulders. A fairly handsome man with nearly black hair and brilliant green eyes. A long, thin scar marred his left cheek from his temple clear to his chin. Carissa had often wondered about that scar. She shook her thoughts away and returned to the subject at hand. "Michael is innocent." This defi-nitely got Daniel's attention, if the raised eyebrows were any indication.

He looked over her clothing again, noting who they really belonged to. She could see his nose flare slightly as he drew in her scent.

Oh yes, he would smell Michael on her. Plus a few other things that would raise odd questions.

"And where is he now?"

"Safe." Carissa met his eyes. She could see the desire to believe her words there, but she could also see doubt. Unzipping her jacket partway, Carissa pulled the file out. "I think this may help." She held the envelope out for him.

Daniel took the package and opened it. "What is it?"

"Michael's last mission files." Carissa waited as Daniel poured over the results Michael had laid out for him.

Distress crossed his face as he read on. "If this is true, we have a serious problem." Daniel flipped over the next page, reading the report.

"As if the problem wasn't serious before this," Carissa scoffed.

Daniel just shook his head slowly and closed the file. "I have a few questions." He laid his hand on top of the closed file. "Please don't take offense to this, but how do I know that Michael isn't forcing you to do this?"

"He's not," Carissa answered.

Daniel considered her for a long moment before letting out a deep sigh. "Where is he?"

"Safe, but he's willing to come in to talk if you can assure he'll remain so." Carissa looked towards the door. "A few of your men seemed a bit upset when I mentioned him."

Daniel laughed heartily. "A bit upset" was probably a slight understatement. "It would help his case greatly if he turned himself in." Daniel sighed. "But, if what you have here is true, that might be an issue. See, this person volunteered to head up the hunt for Michael."

"Michael was afraid of that." Carissa let out an ironic laugh. "If I make arrangements to bring him in—to you—can you assure me his safety?"

"He still has a lot to answer for." Daniel considered her for a moment before nodding his head. "Yes. Bring him in, and I will make sure he's safe."

Carissa mulled over his answer, but movement under her coat made up her mind. Michael obviously trusted this man. "Do you have a spare set of clothing?" She stood up from her chair.

"Of course." Most dragons kept at least one change for emergencies.

"May I have them?"

Daniel gave her an odd look but retrieved a uniform from the bottom drawer of his desk.

It would be too small for Michael, but it would be just a bit large on her. Opening her coat the rest of the way, Carissa let Michael crawl onto Daniel's desktop.

Daniel's mouth hung open as he took in the small, white dragon. Looking from the dragon to Carissa and back, he started to speak, but stopped.

Amusement lit Carissa's eyes as Daniel impersonated a goldfish out of water.

After about the sixth time of trying to start,

he finally settled on, "I see," and sat down. Which didn't make much sense. It was obvious Daniel didn't fully comprehend the situation.

"Michael?" he finally asked.

Michael nodded his head.

"He can't talk right now. I have his voice," Carissa added.

"I see." Daniel just sat there and stared at the dragon on his desk.

Carissa picked up the uniform and quietly changed clothing. Obviously, Daniel needed a moment to wrap his mind around this.

If dragons could smile, Michael's grin would have been ear to ear. Daniel was not an easy man to surprise. He had been around long enough to have seen damn near everything, but this clearly astonished him. Michael stretched his wings before folding them neatly to his back. He sat up on his haunches and wrapped his tail around his feet like he had seen Daniel do so many times.

"Michael?" Daniel asked again.

Michael crossed his front legs over his chest, another trick of Daniel's, and nodded his head again. He could see his boss's mind slowly kicking back into gear.

"White."

Michael nodded.

Daniel's hands shot out and grabbed him. Michael tried to squeak in protest as his boss flipped him around, looking at him as if he had never seen a dragon before. "Tufted tail!" Daniel didn't quite yank on his tail, but it was close. "Boned frill!" The pressure of Daniel's fingers on the back of Michael's head was almost painful. "*Horns!*" Daniel finally held him out at arm's length, looking into his face. "*But white!*"

Michael could understand Daniel's distress.

Dragons all shared the same fundamental shape, but each color had its own, distinct trait. Green dragons, like Daniel, were sleek and smooth from nose to tail. Blue dragons sported backward-sloping horns. Red dragons had tufted tails. Black dragons were graced with a boned frill. But it was the royal, gold dragons, the ones directly descended from the original king, that sported all the traits.

"Not white," Carissa added.

Both men looked over at her.

"What?" Daniel asked, not processing things well.

"He's not white. His scales lack color."

This comment had Daniel flopping Michael around again, inspecting his scales.

157

"Translucent," Daniel muttered, holding Michael almost upside down while looking at his wings. "What have you done?"

Carissa came over and gently took Michael from Daniel's hands, righting him.

He purred silently as she rubbed him under the wings. God, he loved the way she touched him.

"Your clothes are behind the desk." Carissa set him down on the floor. "Get changed."

Michael rubbed his shoulder against her ankle before heading around the desk to shift. He could feel Daniel's eyes as he disappeared behind the desk. *Oh, this is going to be good.*

Michael's shift came easier this time. No pain or waiting to relax, just thinking human and letting go. He could really get used to this. A snicker slipped out of him. He was going to have to get used to it. Carissa had already told him the change couldn't be undone. Rubbing his hand through his hair, he sat up and looked over the desk at Daniel.

"*White!*" Daniel squeaked upon seeing Michael's hair.

For a man of magic, Daniel sure wasn't taking this well. Michael bit back a smile for the moment and reached for the clothing Carissa had left. Mmmm, they were still warm. And they smelled of *Mine!*. Ignoring his inner voice, Michael breathed in a great lungful of that sweet scent as he dragged his shirt on. God, they smelled good together. Once dressed, he stood up to face his boss.

"Michael?" Daniel questioned. He was starting to recover.

Michael mouthed a response, but no sound came out.

"Oh, wait." Carissa stepped up to him and tipped her head back so he could have his voice.

The soft press of her lips called to that part Michael hadn't smacked down. Uncontrollably, his arms pulled her in against him, and he deepened the kiss. She melted against him. It took a moment of exploring her mouth for his conscious mind to wrestle control back. Pulling away, he looked into her eyes. They were molten gold with desire. God, he wanted to swipe everything off the desktop and have her right there. Tempting. His blood raced south, and her eyes widened as she noticed the change in his body.

Placing her hands on his chest, she pushed him away slightly.

Was that a blush on her cheeks? It only made him want to follow through with his idea, but he let her go and turned to his flabbergasted boss. He should apologize for that scene, but he didn't. He was not sorry at all. "Daniel." Michael acknowledged

his boss. Now was probably not a good time to re-
peat the snarky comment he had mouthed earlier.
His inner dragon was screaming at him. He had let
Mine! loose, unclaimed, in a room with another virile,
male dragon. Although she was better, she had been
hurt recently *and* was missing a scale. A scale *he* had
pulled off. He had to protect her.

Unable to completely deny the instincts
pressing on the back of his mind, Michael reached
out and pulled Carissa back towards him. He shifted around, so his body was between her and Daniel.
The feel of her at his back soothed that inner voice
a little. His arm wrapped around to hold her there,
protected. Not quite claimed, but it would have to
do.

Daniel's eyebrow crawled nearly to his hairline as he looked at Michael's positioning. He drew
in a deep breath, testing the air. "Brooding?" Concern raced across Daniel's face as he sampled the
musk and hormones Michael was giving off.

There had to be a real cocktail of interesting
stuff bouncing around the office by now. "It's been
a long week." Michael sighed and dropped his hand
away from Carissa. He had to get his instincts under
control. He trusted Daniel. Daniel was here to help.
Daniel had a steady girlfriend and was not interested
in *Mine!*.

And Carissa is not Mine!*, so shut the hell up!* Michael shook his head, trying to stop the argument going on in his brain. It didn't work very well.

Daniel considered him for a moment before nodding his acceptance of the situation. "Report, Duncan."

Now *this* was the Daniel that Michael knew, the no-nonsense, military man who ran the finest outfit in the world. Michael came to attention and delivered his verbal report.

Chapter Fifteen

LEANING HER CHEEK AGAINST MICHAEL'S BACK, CARISSA felt the rumble of his voice as he laid out his findings for Daniel. There was a tension in him that had nothing to do with the military stance he had assumed. Rubbing her hand down his back, she felt it ease slightly. She should have known. His dragon had claimed her. She let out a long sigh. All the signs were there, but she hadn't been paying close enough attention.

Carissa thought back over the time they'd spent together. His reactions must be pure instinct. She was pretty sure he hadn't made any conscious decision to pursue her. Most of the men who came calling were only interested in her for the power and status she could give them. And those that didn't know who she was, which was rare indeed, skedaddled when they found out who her brother was. Michael didn't seem like a man hunting for power, nor had that last kiss been something she could have shared with someone afraid of her brother. She had meant for it to be a simple exchange, but wow! She still tingled inside from it. Had Daniel not been watching, things would have definitely ended differently.

And, if that weren't enough, Michael had provided for her. A roll at Darien's table. Clothing from his home. Sure, those were either good manners or necessities, but he had also raided Terrence's refrigerator to make her breakfast. Terrence had grumbled while Michael cooked up the last of the eggs and bacon. Michael even made sure she had eaten her fill before starting in on his plate. Carissa hadn't considered that move because he had been explaining his plan at the time, but he hadn't even touched his food until she'd pushed her plate back. Even then, he asked if she'd had enough. Totally missed it. It had been too long since she had been around a mated pair. The male always made sure his lady had enough, was warm enough, and was protected. Michael probably didn't even realize he was doing it.

If his dragon had claimed her, it made perfect sense why he had gone all protective with Daniel but not Terrence. Terrence was human, and therefore not a threat, while Daniel was a dragon in authority, one that Michael took directions from. The delicacy of the situation washed over her, leaving her stunned. She had to find a way to warn Daniel before he tried to separate them. Things could, potentially, get very ugly.

Carissa peeked around Michael's shoulder and tried to catch Daniel's eyes. The man was very intent on Michael's description of their escape. After a few moments, though, his eyes found her. She implored him to catch the not-so-subtle signs she had missed. She felt Michael tense back up when he realized Daniel was no longer focused solely on him. His hand slipped back to her arm and urged her back behind him again. Carissa held Daniel's attention for a moment longer before letting Michael hide her away again. Hopefully, he understood. She turned her head and rubbed her other cheek into his back, easing the tension that had built up there.

"That's very interesting," Daniel paused while he considered the story, "but that doesn't explain how you ended up on video kidnapping Carissa."

Carissa leaned into Michael, giving him her support.

"I honestly don't know." Michael let out a deep sigh.

Carissa's mind had been working on just that thing for a while now. She could only think of one thing. It would explain why their kidnappers had kept Michael alive and not killed him outright. It would have taken a grand mage to do it, but it was

164

not completely impossible. Carissa stepped away from Michael's back so she could join the conversation. Michael tried to hide her away, but she pushed his hands back.

Grabbing him by the front of his shirt, she slammed into his lips, stealing his voice, and pushed him back before he could deepen the kiss. This was not the time to enjoy that particular exchange.

Michael stumbled back, slightly shocked, as she turned to Daniel.

"Can I see this video?" Carissa ignored Michael as he regained his footing and slipped his hand to her lower back, reinforcing his unspoken claim on her. She should turn around and smack him down, but his touch just felt so good. She would have to deal with him soon, but later.

"Of course." Daniel shifted his chair closer to the wrong side of his desk and twisted his laptop around so he could access it. "There." He hit a few buttons and moved the screen so Carissa and Michael could see it. They watched as what was obviously Michael carried Carissa's limp form out of a door and dropped her in the back of a van.

Anger radiated off Michael as he growled soundlessly. His mouth worked, and he voicelessly protested the video.

Carissa shushed him and restarted the video.

She rested her palms on the desk and leaned in so she could see the picture better. There was something about it that bothered her.

Unable to make any other noise, Michael clicked his tongue loudly against his teeth and stabbed his finger at the image of Carissa's limp form. His fingers curled against her back in agitation.

"What?" Carissa turned her attention up to Michael. He mouthed a word that brought her head spinning back to the video. She restarted it again and studied their figures before letting out a bark of laughter. Carissa stood up and waved her hand at the video.

"That isn't Michael." She smiled at the confusion on Daniel's face. "That isn't even me." How could whoever had copied them have gotten it so wrong?

"*What?*" Daniel spun the computer around and replayed the video. "That is most definitely you." He studied the limp woman.

Carissa laughed and pointed to the woman's dress. "It may look like me, but it isn't. My dress was gold with bronze filigree. This dress is bronze with gold filigree."

Daniel's eyes worked over the picture again. "Are you sure?" There was a note of hope mixed in with the disbelief in his voice.

166

"Oh yes." Carissa smiled and nodded. "It took me nearly three months to get that fabric. The company kept sending the bronze with gold." Carissa paused as she thought about the numerous complaints she'd made about receiving the wrong material. "I had a dress made of the wrong stuff for a function a few months ago because I had to, but I wore the gold with bronze filigree to this ball. I was so excited that I'd finally gotten the one I wanted." She paused again as something else struck her. "And come to think of it, where's the curtain?" Carissa looked at the still image again.

Michael caressed her back and nodded his head in agreement.

Daniel looked up from the image to Carissa. "Curtain?"

"I woke up wrapped in one of the curtains from Baron Estivis' main sitting room." Carissa looked up to where Michael was nodding his agreement. She looked back to Daniel. "There's no curtain here. Does Michael go back in after putting me in the van?"

"No." Daniel shook his head and sped through the video. "He just gets in the van and drives off."

"Then how did I get wrapped up in the curtain?" Carissa asked.

Daniel zipped through the video a few times,

thinking. "Then how do you explain this video?" He looked up, waiting.

Carissa smiled at him. There was only one possibility. "Doppelgangers." Her smile got toothy. "Very inattentive doppelgangers, at that." It was the only reason she could see for them keeping Michael alive. If they wanted to frame him for her abduction, the mage casting the spell would need a living subject to image from.

A light clicked on in Daniel as he put things together. "And, if we thought Michael was responsible for your abduction, then we would be more likely to believe he was also responsible for the other disappearances." Daniel rolled his head back and looked up at the ceiling in exasperation. "We would never have even looked elsewhere for the real culprits. How could I be so blind?" He tipped his head forwards and looked at Michael.

"I am sorry, Michael." Daniel genuinely sounded remorseful. "Jareth brought forth such a compelling case, and with Carissa's abduction and that video, I didn't think to question the logic."

"And what are you going to do about that?" Carissa asked the question she was sure was running through Michael's head.

Daniel let out a breathy sigh. "I'm going to arrest him." He looked over the file and the video.

"But this is going to make life hard."

"How so?" Carissa asked. The facts were all laid out for anyone to see.

"I have two files on the same case. Two opposing views, and each points at the other very convincingly," Daniel pointed out. "And the fact that Michael kidnapped you a second time."

"He did *not* kidnap me!" Carissa hissed.

Daniel's eyebrows did those pushups again. "Maybe not, but you did disappear and were later seen in his company," Daniel replied. "Your brother is absolutely furious at the moment, which does not bode well for Michael's case." He looked up at the clock. "And he should be getting here at any moment." As if by magic, a pounding came from Daniel's door, followed by Carissa's name in a *very* angry voice.

This was bad.

"Shit," Daniel cursed as he stood up to face the hammering.

They only had a few moments before her brother broke that door down. If they were ever going to prove Michael's innocence, they had to get out of there *now.* Carissa turned and grabbed Michael, pulling his attention from the weakening door. "Shift!"

Michael nodded and slipped into dragon form.

Carissa grabbed him up and rushed to the window.

"He'll never make it out." Daniel had followed her. "Not even dragons can make it off the property."

Carissa knew about the safety measures used to secure Eternity's main headquarters. "He doesn't have to." She yanked open the window and set Michael on the ledge. "Please," Carissa turned back to Daniel, "make my brother understand." Without giving him a chance to respond, Carissa shifted to dragon form and jumped up to the window. The creak of wood sounded from the door.

"No, Carissa," Daniel protested.

"Once he understands, tell him I'll be waiting for him." Carissa shouldered Michael and jumped off the ledge.

Michael followed in a beat of wings.

"Where?" Daniel yelled after them.

"He'll know." Carissa's answer was almost lost in the roar her brother let out as he finally broke into Daniel's office.

Terror coursed through Michael's veins as he beat his wings, trying to keep up with Carissa's pointless flight. A second roar had announced the king's shift to dragon form. Thankfully, he had to shift in Daniel's office, making it impossible to transform into his grand dragon state, but that didn't mean the small dragon form wouldn't be deadly enough. Yay, torn to pieces versus roasted alive! And then there were the magical barriers in place to secure the area. They might as well give up. They were only making their plight worse.

Michael wanted to stop, to turn himself in, but something inside him forced him to frantically chase Carissa. They were being pursued by an insanely mad dragon, and Carissa was injured. He had to protect *Mine!*. Michael caught up with Carissa as she slowed slightly. He nipped at her tail as it swished past his face. They needed to go if they held any hopes of finding a safe place to hide. As it was, they were coming up on the edge of the property.

Suddenly, Carissa flipped in air, landing right on Michael's back.

What the hell?

She folded up her wings, and they dropped like a stone.

He flapped vainly, but she had grabbed onto his wings, hampering his ability to move. Michael rolled, trying to get her off, but she clung to him. They were only feet from solid concrete! Michael opened his mouth in a silent scream as they collided with the ground… and it gave way under him. Water rushed into his mouth as Carissa's wings shot out and pulled them both to the surface of a lake that hadn't been there a moment before.

Carissa turned Michael loose as his head broke the water.

He thrashed about for a few moments until he realized his wings were more of a hindrance then help. Tucking them back before he drowned, he dog-paddled for all he was worth. His eyes tracked Carissa as she glided through the water. *Crazy woman!* She moved surprisingly quickly as she swam circles around him. How the hell did she move so quickly? He watched her graceful form pass his face again. Hell, she wasn't even using her legs. *Tail!* She was using her tail.

Michael was rewarded with a burst of momentum as he flicked his tail back and forth. Great! He might actually live through this… just to be massacred by Carissa's brother. Why had she insisted on them running?

Seeing that he had figured out how to swim, Carissa rubbed up along his side and shot for the shore.

Michael snorted and followed a few lengths behind her. She was going to have some explaining to do.

Carissa had already shaken off and was curled in the warm sand by the time Michael dragged his carcass from the water. Michael shook himself, shedding water droplets before turning his anger towards Carissa. He yelled at her—or would have, if he'd had a voice. Pacing the sand in front of her, he let go with the rough side of his tongue. Sure, she couldn't hear it, but she would get the fact that he was mad at her, and it made him feel better. Was that amusement in her eyes? Did she find this funny? They could have been killed! He stuck his face into hers and growled at her.

The end of Carissa's tail thwaped down on top of his head, knocking his chin into the sand. A clawed foot followed, pressing his head down. "*One—*" Carissa snapped at him, "—you do not talk to me that way!" She pressed harder on him, emphasizing her point. "Only my *mate* has the right to talk to me like that, and you have no claim on me!"

Michael's inner voice writhed in agony at the truth in her words.

"My brother doesn't even talk to me like that!"

Michael went limp under her claws. She was right; he really shouldn't have blown up at her like that.

Seeing he had gone limp, Carissa shoved his head away, making Michael roll onto his side. Now she paced, yelling at him. Only she had the voice to do so. "*Second*—what the hell do you have to be mad about? I just saved your sorry ass!"

Michael lay there, taking his tongue lashing.

"We had to get out of there. My brother was not in a listening mood." She let out a deep breath and flopped down on the sand. She was perpendicular to Michael's sprawled form with her nose almost touching his. "We had to go. Give Daniel a little time to work. He was always good at handling my brother when he was in a tiff." She sounded so forlorn.

Michael shifted so they lay together.

Carissa leaned against him. "I'm sorry that I didn't warn you before we shifted space." She let out another noisy breath. "I suppose that was your first time."

Michael paused for a moment before nodding his head. What did she mean, 'shift space'? He opened his mouth to ask, but closed it again. There was no point. He snorted again and leaned into her. Goodness, she felt good against him. He was going to miss her warmth when this was over. His inner voice screamed at him, but he smacked it down with a note of finality that silenced it. She already told him he didn't have a claim to her. He was just going to have to find a way to deal with it.

"Let's go." Carissa sighed and pushed her way

up from the soft sand. "It's not far."

Michael heaved himself up and followed her. Life's simple truths had left him rather depressed. He was a hunted man, drawn to a woman he had no rights to. As soon as this whole sordid affair was over, she would go back to her world of high society. Hell, she probably had dozens of suitors waiting for her return. She might even have a lover somewhere. That thought depressed him even more. And he, well, he was likely out of a job.

Even if Daniel could clear this mess up, his coworkers would always look at him suspiciously. Then there was the whole split-personality thing. How could he handle missions with a voice in the back of his mind, feeding him commentary? Some of it went strictly against what he needed to do.

Michael let out another snort as he decided. Once this was over and his name was cleared, he'd resign. He'd pack up anything left from his ruined home, hop on his Harley, and hit the road. It didn't matter where he went, life as he knew it was already over. Surprisingly, the voice in his head remained morbidly silent.

Chapter Sixteen

THE SIGHT CARISSA SAW WHEN SHE PEEKED BACK OVER her shoulder confused her. Michael looked so forlorn. The tips of his wings scraped across the ground as he pulled himself forwards. His tail hung limply behind him, and his nose was just barely held above the dirt path. What did the man have to be depressed about? They had escaped unharmed. Daniel believed them. He could convince Kyle of Michael's innocence. They could then arrest the one responsible, and things could go back to the way they were supposed to be.

But, they couldn't. Carissa's mind churned as they walked. Michael was a different person now. Sure, he was adjusting to his new nature, but it would be a while before he had that under control. And his good name had been dragged through the mud. Oh, that could make people not trust him, even if he were innocent. Ouch. She pondered the other changes in his life. His ruined home. That bit of his psyche his instincts had hijacked. What if he had a girlfriend? That thought brought a growl rumbling up from Carissa's chest. She didn't like the idea of someone else having a claim on him. Whoever this mystery chick was, she was going to have a fight on her hands whenever this was over. Carissa wasn't going to let him go that easily.

What? Carissa stopped dead in her tracks as she processed the thought that passed through her mind. Her instincts had just staked a claim on Michael! How could she be so stupid? She had just reprimanded Michael for acting like her mate, and here she was, trying to claim him. In his brooding state, having her reject him like she had may account for part of his overwhelming depression. Her tail thrashed in anger at herself, and the fringy end whapped Michael in the side of the head, knocking him over.

Carissa squeaked as she spun around to check on Michael. His eyes were closed as he lay crumpled in the dirt. All the fight had gone out of him. She hadn't hit him that hard, had she? Shifting to human, she bent over the sprawled form.

"I am so sorry." Carissa felt his side to make sure he was breathing. He rumbled lightly under her fingers but didn't move. Okay, so she hadn't killed him with her tail. He was just giving up on life. That was almost as bad. She was going to have to do something to bring that fire back into him. It hurt her heart to see him so down.

"Come on." She carefully lifted him up to rest against her shoulder. He hung there, limp as a water-starved plant. "It's not that bad." She patted his back as she stood up. There was only a little bit farther to go.

Michael snorted a warm puff of air into her hair.

"Just give Daniel a little time to bring Kyle around. That will solve half the problems." Maybe. "I'm sure the two of them can figure out a way to clear your name with the information we gave them." Possibly.

Michael squirmed against her, scratching her with the points of his claws.

"Shhhh." She petted him soothingly as she headed towards the small cabin tucked away in the woods.

Carissa cuddled Michael to her as she dug out the keys to the cabin. Only she and her brother knew about this place. They had both gone to great lengths to make sure Eternity didn't discover it. It wasn't much, but it had served as Carissa's private getaway for those times when the world had finally gotten to be too much for her. She crossed the small living room to the couch and placed Michael on the center.

"Why don't you shift back while I go find something to wear?" Carissa turned from him and headed back down the hall. She didn't mind being naked around him, but Michael's depression had triggered her protective instincts. She just wanted to cuddle him close and make sure he was okay, and that would work a whole lot better if they were both dressed. Although, staying naked was one surefire way to break him out of his funk. She considered it for a moment as she pulled out clothing, a flowing gown for her and one of her brother's robes for Michael. Then, if things *did* turn hot and heavy, there wouldn't be much to get out of the way. Wow, she really needed to get her mind back up to a civilized level and stop thinking about ways she could distract Michael from his problems. Carissa pushed that thought away as she slipped into her dress.

"The only men's clothing I have is my brother's," Carissa said as she came back out with the robe. "He's about your size, so I think it will fit." Her eyes fell to the little, white lump on her couch. "Now come on." She came over and sat on the couch next to him. "I know things look bleak, but that's no reason to give up." She rubbed her hand down Michael's back. When he didn't respond, she lifted him up, forcing him to look into her eyes. "I know you're innocent."

Michael rumbled halfheartedly and let his head drop down, away from her eyes.

Carissa let out a sigh and leaned back against the sofa. She set Michael down so his head rested on her shoulder and his body draped down her chest. "It may not matter to you, but I want you to know that I do care what happens," Carissa confessed as she caressed his back. "I won't let them railroad you for something you didn't do." She paused, thinking about his situation. "If worse comes to worst, you can stay here. Only Kyle and I know about this place. Eternity won't find you here. I promise, no matter what happens, I won't abandon you." She would find a way to convince her brother to do something to help him. Hell, she'd beat it out of him if she had to.

Shifting into the corner of the couch, Carissa relaxed back under Michael's weight. She ran her fingers over him, taking in the texture of his scales and rubbing in all those little spots that she liked to be rubbed. It wasn't long until he vibrated with a silent purr, and the tip of his tall flipped back and forth, showing signs of contentment. Good. He might still be somewhat depressed, but he wasn't scraping the bottom of the barrel anymore. Carissa sighed and sat up, holding him against her.

"If you'll excuse me, I need to go take a bath."

Carissa slipped Michael down on the warm cushion. "I'm rather overdue for a good soaking." Making sure he curled back up, she scratched his head one last time. "If you feel like changing back, here are clothes," she said and dropped her brother's robe over the arm of the sofa, "and there is food in the kitchen if you get hungry. I'll just be in the other room if you need me." She looked at him for a moment before dropping a kiss on his head and walking out. It had been a few days since her last bath, and she was dying for a good scrubbing.

Michael curled into the warmth Carissa had left behind as he watched her head down the hall to the bathroom. Man, what a fantastic view.

See, you do *have a chance,* Michael's peanut gallery poked at him. Now it decided to speak up.

Yeah right, Michael pushed back. *She's way out of my league.*

But Mine! *said she wouldn't leave us.*

She's not Mine!, Michael growled. How many times did he have to tell that wayward bit that he didn't own her?

But, she could *be,* it pushed back.

This made Michael pause. She did say she

cared, and she had just spent a fair amount of time rubbing on him. His scales still tingled from her gentle kneading. How did she know just where to touch? Her slow caresses had worked out most of the bitterness he was feeling towards the world. He let out a puff of air, conceding the potential. His inner dragon danced with joy.

Ignoring the giddy spot in the back of his brain, Michael looked around the small cabin. It was sparsely furnished in a rustic way, but there was a touch of femininity that softened the edges. Very comfortable. The only things that weren't sparse were the bookshelves. They covered nearly every open wall and were jam-packed with books and scrolls of every type. Michael had never seen so many old books together outside of a library. What was this place?

The sounds of running water drew Michael's attention, making his dragon perk up. The thought of Carissa stripping out of that flowing dress and dipping into bubble-filled water made him squirm. He fought with the desire to go investigate. He would not go spy on her all wet and naked.

Is Mine! *safe?* his peanut gallery piped in.

Of course Mine! *is safe. And her name is Carissa, not* Mine!, Michael snapped back.

Are you sure?

Michael paused in his quick comeback. Carissa was safe. She had to be. This was her place. And she said that no one but Kyle knew about it. A loud bang came from the bathroom, freezing Michael's heart. *Mine! was* safe, wasn't she?

Driven by sudden apprehension, Michael slipped off the couch and scurried down the hall towards where Carissa had gone. He paused at the open door, debating. He couldn't see anything in the center of the room. Only a white bathroom mat. Should he continue? The dragon part of him pushed him on. *Mine!* could've fallen in the tub; she could be bleeding out even as he debated. The thought of her dying pushed him forwards into the room.

An old, claw-footed tub took up one entire side of the room. *Mine!* sat waist-deep in bubbly water, fussing with what looked to be a shelf on a pole. Several bottles floated in the water as she secured the end of the pole to the edge of the tub again. Michael let out a deep sigh of relief as the tightness around his heart eased. *Mine!* was safe. Before he could shift back to human, she finished with the shelf and started gathering up the bottles. Michael relaxed down to the rug and watched her move. So elegant, so smooth, so perfect. He would do anything for her.

Michael's breath slowed as he processed his train of thought. Had that come from his rampant dragon part, or from someplace else? His peanut gallery laughed and shook its head at him. That part would have served her from the moment it saw her, so this new revelation hadn't come from it. Was Michael, the man, actually falling in love with her? Or, was it just hormones?

Mine! let out a deep breath, drawing Michael's attention away from his thoughts. From his point of view, all he could really see was the profile of her face where she relaxed back into the water. Her eyes were closed, and she breathed softly through parted lips. Oh, those lips looked so kissable.

Turning from that heavenly sight, Michael slipped from the room, unseen. The last few days had been hard on *Mine!,* and she deserved to relax a little. Maybe he should see about scrounging up something to eat. Michael jumped up to the couch to shift back to human form. His exploration would be easier that way. Then he could make *Mine!* something nice and offer to scrub her back, among other things. He let his mind go, but that tickle of magic that came with shifting didn't start. Michael shook his head, clearing away thoughts of *Mine!* writhing under his hands and concentrated on being human. Nothing! Of all the times his dragon could chose to be stubborn, *why now?*

This was not an uncommon event in the life of dragons. Every now and then, a dragon would

184

find that his parts were too far out of sync to transform. There were support groups set up to help those individuals find their balance. Having worked with the solitary dragons list, Michael had taken more than one unfortunate dragon in for help. He knew the process, but he had never thought he would ever need to use it.

Drawing in a deep breath, Michael pushed his front legs forwards and his back legs backwards. He extended his wings out as wide as they would go and straightened his tail, stretching all of his muscles. Relaxing into the cushions, Michael searched inside himself for the feel of being human. He should know it. He had been human most of his life.

The reptilian part of him laughed at him.

And what's so funny? Michael asked it.

You need to explore your dragon side more, it laughed.

Michael snorted. As if he weren't *already* exploring his dragon side. He needed to get back to human so he could explore that side with *Mine!*. He pushed the snickering voice away and thought about all the things that made him human. It was hard to concentrate with scales rubbing against the back of his mind. No wonder some dragons had a hard time shifting back when they got stuck.

Not going to work, his insides teased in a singsong voice.

If he could have, Michael would have pounded that smirk right out of that wayward bit. That type of commentary was not helping. Ignoring the taunting voice was not getting him anywhere closer to human.

Fine! Michael let out another snort and turned his mind to that voice. If it wanted to speak, he would listen. Until he discovered what his instincts wanted him to know, there was no way he would be able to change back.

17

Being clean is magnificent! Carissa sighed as she pulled the wet towel from her head. She had kind of hoped that Michael would have come in to join her. She had left the bathroom door open in hopes that he would catch the hint, but he hadn't. Carissa slipped back into her dress and went to find him. She smiled when her eyes spotted the white mass stretched out on the couch. Michael covered two full cushions on the couch. Man, he was long for his size. But what did she expect? Both she and her brother were long in dragon form.

"Hey there." Carissa spoke softly as she approached. "Did you have a nice nap?" Her fingers slid over his wings.

Michael cracked an eye and looked up at her.

He opened his mouth, but no sound came out. He seemed frustrated by this inability to respond.

"It's all right," Carissa reassured him as he tucked in his bits. "How about we see about some food?"

Michael nodded at this.

Carissa scooped him up and placed him on her shoulder before heading to the small kitchen space. "So what do you feel like?" They perused the refrigerator. There wasn't a lot of fresh food, but the freezer was well stocked.

"This looks good." Carissa pulled out a couple of frozen steaks and some broccoli with cheese.

Michael nodded heartily.

Good. A couple of minutes in the microwave, and it should be thawed enough to broil. "Why don't you sit here?" Carissa moved Michael to the counter next to the stove. "That way, you can help with the seasoning."

Michael carefully circled on the counter so his tail was tucked up out of the way.

Carissa busied herself with thawing the meat. A loud bang from the front of the cabin drew both of their attention.

"*Carissa!*" a loud voice bellowed as the door swung open. Kyle stood, seething, in the opening.

Carissa whipped around to face him, but she

shifted over so Michael was out of sight. Apparently, Daniel hadn't been able to handle her brother. But, at least he'd had the good sense to show up dressed.

"Brother!"

"*Where is he?*" Kyle stormed into the room, looking around for Michael. "I want that no-good son of a bitch!" He stopped a few paces away from Carissa, eyes searching the living room area. "He will pay dearly for what he has done!"

Oh, this was not good.

"Did you talk to Daniel?" Carissa tried to use a soothing voice on her brother.

Kyle glared at her. "You're protecting him, aren't you?" he growled. "How could you, after what he's done?"

"Did you talk to Daniel?" Carissa asked again, less calm than she had been. Kyle's attitude was starting to tick her off.

"*What the hell does he have to do with this?*" Kyle yelled.

That did it. "Did. You. Talk. To. Daniel?"

"Yes, I talked to Daniel!" Kyle threw his hands up and turned away from Carissa to prowl around the living space.

"Did he show you the file?"

"Yes, he showed me the file."

"So, you know Michael is innocent." Carissa

gave her brother one more chance to calm down.

"I don't *care* if he's innocent. He kidnapped you!" Kyle growled, stalking back over, getting into Carissa's face.

Oh, *this* was how it was going to be? Carissa's patience snapped. "*First!*" she barked into her brother's face, "*you do not talk to me that way!*" She raised a finger and shoved it into his chest, pushing him back. "I don't care if you *are* the bloody *king*, you are my *brother! Not* my *mother, not* my *mate*—my *brother!* And by now, you should know that *no one* talks to me that way!"

Some of the starch went out of Kyle as he backed up. Carissa was something when furious.

"*Second!* Michael did *not* kidnap me! If anything, I kidnapped him. Both times, it was my idea to leave. Hell, I had to throw the man off the building and pray his instincts kicked in before he hit the ground. And *he* wanted to turn himself in to Daniel. I was the one that dragged him out here."

Carissa stalked after her brother as he backed across the room. "*Damn it,* Kyle!" Carissa backed him clear into the living room. "He was only doing his goddamn job!"

She took a breath to calm down slightly. "He was in your service when they kidnapped him. They locked him in a dungeon. Chained him to a wall. No food. No water. Unable to even sit down. *Chained* to a *wall!* Do you hear me?"

Carissa paused, so her brother could nod, dumbfounded.

"And *then*, when he *does* get out, is he welcomed home? *No!* He's accused of crimes and hunted like a dog. Did you ever stop to think before you sent your henchmen after him? Did you see what they did to his home? Destroyed! Completely and utterly destroyed! They didn't just toss it—they tore up damn near everything in it. Then, I…" Carissa drew in a deep breath. "I screwed his life up even more." She shook her head at what she had done before turning her attention back to her brother. "But, you, *you* didn't even give him the benefit of the doubt."

Her anger flamed again as she went on. "And now, you have the *nerve* to come out here, demanding that I hand him over. After having heard his case. *Seeing* the evidence! And you call yourself a *king?* *How dare you!* You're nothing but a three-footed, webbed-winged…"

Carissa's mouth moved as she continued to insult Kyle, but her anger had burned through the magic holding Michael's voice. A smirk broke out across Kyle's face, inflaming Carissa's anger even more. Reaching out, she grabbed the front of his shirt and slammed her lips to his, stealing his voice.

"*This is not a laughing matter!*" she screamed at him.

Shock raced across Kyle's face. She rarely borrowed his voice. And she *never* took it without asking. His knees caught the edge of the couch, and he went down.

She glared at him as he sat on the couch. "You want Michael? *Fine!*" Carissa turned and stormed back into the kitchen. Michael tried to scamper away from the raging woman, but she snatched him up. "*Fine!*" she yelled again as she stormed back to her shocked brother. "*Here!*" She dumped the little dragon into her brother's lap.

Kyle's hands came up to keep Michael from falling off.

"Don't you *dare* hurt one goddamn scale on his hide! *Do you hear me? He's mine!* And if you even *think* about asking how he got to be a dragon, you will rue the day you were hatched!"

Carissa turned and stormed out of the cabin, leaving the two men gawking at her. Shifting to grand dragon form, she let out a roar, released Kyle's voice, and leaped into the air. A good, long flight should help calm her nerves. And if Kyle so much as insulted Michael, she'd roast him when she got back.

Carissa's ferocious roar shook the cabin as the two men stared at the swinging door in silence. The sound of her wings ripped through the air as she took to the skies in a tiff. Man, she was loud when she was mad. She was also amazingly gorgeous. Michael drew in a deep, cleansing breath before letting it out slowly. He looked up at the shocked man holding him.

"I never touched her." He chirped as he slipped out of the King's hands and onto the couch next to him. True, he'd thought about it hard and often, but he'd never had the chance to make good on those ideas.

Kyle looked down at the white dragon. Humor washed away the shock on Kyle's face. A slow smile was followed by a deep chuckle. "I'm sure you wouldn't have lived long if you had." Kyle looked back at the door that had come to rest part of the way open. "I'd forgotten she gets feisty when she's mad."

Michael nodded his head in agreement. "I'll remember that."

"Please do." Kyle chuckled. "It may save your life someday." Letting out a cleansing breath, Kyle turned his attention to Michael. "Well, let's have a look at you." He slipped his hands up under Michael's wings and raised the small dragon level with his eyes. "She really did a number on you."

Michael could feel the king's eyes shift from his head clear to his tail. "You're telling me," Michael grumbled, earning another laugh from Kyle. "Right now, I'm stuck."

"Oh, really?" The amusement in Kyle's voice stung.

Michael nodded his head. It sucked having to admit it, but Michael knew the dragon king could help. He had the ability to subdue the dragon part of his subjects, allowing them to transform back to human.

Kyle studied him for a few more moments before setting him on the floor in front of him. "You really need to get more in touch with your dragon side. It will keep this from happening in the future."

Michael snorted his understanding. That was exactly what his instincts had told him. Great. The peanut gallery wins again. Michael bowed his head and waited, while Kyle called forth Michael's dragon and suppressed it. The tingle of magic washed over Michael, leaving him kneeling, naked, on the floor.

Kyle handed him the robe Carissa had set out.

Slipping it over his head, Michael stood up. "Thank you." God this was awkward. What was he supposed to do now? Scrape and bow? Michael had met the king many times in his line of work, but the man had always been regal and respectable. It was hard to respect someone who had come to kill you, and that rumpled shirt and jeans were far from regal. Watching him be chewed up by his sister hadn't helped, either. Man, she had one hell of a temper on her. Just the thought of the fire flashing in her eyes had Michael's nether regions sitting up to take notice. *And* on *that* note…

Michael turned away from the king to tend to the meat Carissa had pulled out. "We were going to have steaks. Would you care to join us?" Michael fussed with the microwave, trying to distract himself. Why did he have to get hard at the worst possible times?

"Sure," Kyle answered. He stood up to pull another steak out of the freezer.

Well, at least the man knew his way around a kitchen.

The two men worked in silence as they thawed and seasoned the meat. Sticking it under the hot broiler, Kyle finally turned to Michael. "So," his voice sounded apprehensive, "you had nothing to do with any of it?"

Michael let out a sigh. "No."

"And Carissa's disappearance from her room?"

"Hey." Michael felt a little upset about that. "She's the one that tossed me off the building." Had she really said she'd hoped his instincts would kick in before he hit the ground?

Kyle chuckled lightly. "That sounds like something she'd do."

"I really would have preferred if we could have ended this thing when she brought me in to see Daniel." Michael shrugged, not wanting to mention why they ran the second time.

"Point." Kyle sighed, catching the missing accusation. "To be fair, I was worried about her. The guard that called said she looked rough." Kyle turned to lean his backside on the counter as he spoke. "No one hurts my sister and gets away with it."

Michael sighed as he popped the package of broccoli and cheese in the microwave. "I understand that." If Kyle's protective streak ran half as deep as Michael's, someone was really going to pay for kidnapping Carissa. Just the fact that she had taken off by herself was eating at him. But, for once, his peanut gallery and his heart were in total agreement. *Mine!* needed a little space to cool off. If she wasn't back by the time the food was done, he'd go looking for her.

"So," Kyle crossed his arms over his chest and turned a considering eye to Michael, "do you have any ideas about how to clean up this mess?"

Michael paused as he pulled a bowl down for the broccoli. "Maybe." He and his peanut gallery had been working that problem over since shortly after he had stretched out. "But Carissa is not going to like it." Oh no, *Mine!* was definitely not going to like it one bit.

Eighteen

ABSOLUTELY NOT! CARISSA SLAMMED HER CUP DOWN ON the table, showing her displeasure. Her flight had done a lot to soothe her frayed nerves, and she had been delighted to see Michael and her brother deep in conversation when she got back. That was definitely a good sign. But, the plan they had hatched was asinine. How could either of them think this load of asshatery held any merit?

"But, Carissa," Kyle spoke softly, trying to soothe his sister. "This is the perfect solution. We can't just go in there and arrest him without substantial evidence against him."

Carissa gaped at him and pointed to Michael. He had called for Michael's arrest on the same amount of evidence! Carissa was livid.

"No." Kyle shook his head. Years of practice had given him insight into Carissa's thoughts. It wasn't hard to follow her reasoning. "I also have him kidnapping you on video."

Carissa slammed her fist into the table again, mouthing her denial.

"I know that wasn't you," Kyle said, soothing her riled nerves, "but at the time, I didn't. The fact that it looked like you was more than enough to call for his arrest."

"Carissa," Michael said, adding his support to Kyle, "look at it from their point of view. As far as they know, I've disappeared with you three times. Kyle can't just walk in there and say I'm innocent and point his finger at the man accusing me. It's a weak position to be in, and, as king, he can't afford to be weak."

Kyle nodded his agreement.

Carissa shook her head, adamantly against this idea. This was not going to happen.

"Look. Turning myself in publicly is the best way to draw him out." Michael tapped the tip of his finger on the table, trying to drive home his point. "Eternity may manhandle me during the arrest, but they won't really hurt me in a public setting. And once I'm in custody, Daniel will be there to make sure nothing happens."

"He's sure to make a move during the arrest," Kyle added. "He can't afford to let Michael testify. And that, coupled with the evidence we already have, will be enough to arrest him."

198

Carissa shook her head, denying them again. It was going to be over her dead body.

"I know you don't like it." Michael took Carissa's hand and curled it around his. He stroked it gently, trying to soothe her. "But, this is the quickest way to solve the issue."

Carissa clenched her teeth and glared at him. He continued to rub her hand, sending little jolts of electricity up her arm to befuddle her mind. She shook her head in refusal once again, but her will wasn't as strong as it had been a moment ago. She looked from Michael to her brother and back. This was stupid. How could she convince them this was a bad idea? Michael's hand had worked its way up her arm to rub on her bicep. God, his touch felt so good.

"It's the best option we have." Michael caressed her, weakening her resistance.

What if he got hurt? Carissa clutched at the hand she held. How did she make him understand her fears? She had promised herself that she would take care of him. Carissa looked back at her brother, but Kyle was tuned in on Michael. There was a calculating look on his face that Carissa didn't like. She looked back at Michael. What did he see that she did not?

"I'll be fine." His hand had reached her shoulder.

Carissa closed her eyes, enjoying his touch. No. She shook her head one more time.

"Carissa."

The way Michael said her name sent a shiver up Carissa's spine.

"I have to do this." His fingers slid over her shoulder and down her back. "I have to turn myself in. There's no other choice." He rubbed her back gently. "Eternity will not stop until they've chased me down. I can't hide forever. And I would rather go in my way than be cornered somewhere I could get hurt."

This logic, Carissa could not argue with. She could keep him safe for a while, but the longer they hid, the more ferocious Eternity would get. She took one more look at her brother before giving in. *Fine!* She threw up her free hand, signaling her defeat. If he wanted to go get himself shot at, who was she to stop him?

Michael squeezed her hand reassuringly.

But he wasn't going alone. Carissa pointed at herself, then to Michael, then towards the door. That stopped the movement of Michael's fingers.

"*No!*" Both Michael and her brother protested.

She shot them both a wicked grin and nodded her head slowly. If they wanted to play this way, oh, she would play. She made the gesture again, reaffirming her decision.

"Oh no." Kyle sat up, ready to exert his authority.

Carissa grabbed his shirt and stole his voice once again. "And how, pray tell, are you going to explain my absence?" Carissa snapped.

The two men froze as they considered her words.

"I'm supposedly kidnapped. What do you think Eternity would do if he showed up somewhere without me?"

Michael and Kyle looked at each other, worried.

Carissa knew she had a valid point. "Besides, there's less of a chance that they'll shoot if I'm there." The looks that crossed both Michael's and Kyle's faces showed they were expecting just that. She looked from one to the other in shock. Standing up, she threw Michael's hands off her. "You're going in *expecting* to get shot!" How could she be so blind!

She rounded on her brother. "And you were going to let him, knowing this?"

"It's the only way," Michael cooed.

"Fine!" Carissa huffed. "You want to turn yourself in and get shot at… so be it. But I am going with you." She turned and pointed her finger at Kyle. "And not one word from you."

Kyle shut his mouth.

"Just make sure Daniel has a medic on hand, in case things go bad." Turning, she stormed out of the cabin again before they could try to talk her out of it. She was not letting Michael go in there alone. She protected what was hers, and he might not realize it yet, but he was most definitely hers.

Whose stupid idea was this? Michael questioned his logic for about the millionth time. It had made perfect sense for him to let Eternity apprehend him at Central Park. There would be enough witnesses to keep them from open hostility, yet enough space that innocent bystanders wouldn't be drawn in if anything did happen. That was before Carissa had inserted herself into his plans. Oh, her case was sound and her logic undeniable, but he wanted *Mine!* as far away from the action as possible.

"Please, is there any way I can convince you not to do this?" Michael begged again. He knew the answer, but he had to ask.

Carissa just shook her head. This had been the gist of their conversation since Kyle had left last night to make arrangements with Daniel. Carissa hadn't even let Michael touch her after her second

202

fit of anger. He had pleaded with her to change her mind until she threw a pillow at his head and sent him to sleep on the couch. Even though he didn't have a clue where they were, he had tried to slip out in the middle of the night, only to find she had magically sealed the doors. That had gotten another pillow thrown at him.

"Just stay close, then." Michael slipped his hand into hers and pulled her into line with his body. He would do everything in his power to make sure she was safe through this. His dragon protested as they walked out of the bushes and onto the main path. Kyle had informed Daniel that they would make the rounds of the park, waiting for Eternity to show up to arrest him. They would take Carissa to safety, and he would be taken into custody.

Michael's dragon didn't like the idea of *Mine!* being taken from him, but it could not argue that it was the best place for her. Being in Michael's presence put her in a whole lot more danger.

They made two turns of the park together. Even though he was waiting for all hell to break loose, he couldn't help but enjoy himself. He had wrapped his arm around *Mine!*, holding her closer than she had let him last night. Her hand had slipped into the back pocket of the jeans she had dug out for him. Every now and then, her fingers would curl, cupping his ass in a way that made his heart skip. God, she felt good. Eternity had better make their appearance soon, or he was going to abandon this plan and find a nice, secluded spot to give in to that voice yelling in the back of his head.

"Michael Duncan!" an authoritative voice called from behind him. "Hold it right there." Of course they would come at him from behind.

Michael turned to look straight down the barrel of a 9mm Beretta. He knew that gun, and he knew the man holding it. "Hey, Demarco." Michael smiled at him. He shifted so his body was between Carissa and Demarco.

Carissa peeked around him.

"Let her go, Duncan." The clean-cut, black man held his gun level with Michael's heart.

"I don't want any trouble." Michael raised his hands up, away from Carissa.

Demarco shifted his head, checking to make sure Carissa was free. "Please step away from him, Lady Carissa." Demarco's eyes switched between Carissa and Michael.

Movement off to the right drew Michael's attention. Another gun leveled at his heart. His eyes shifted to the left. Two more of his fellow Elites had beads trained on him. Good to know they were taking him as a serious threat.

Carissa slipped her hand out of Michael's pocket and stepped around in front of him. To his utmost amazement, she pressed her back into his front, shielding him from potential bullets.

Demarco reached out his hand for Carissa. "Come on, My Lady," he said, trying to coax her away from him.

She just shook her head and leaned into Michael.

"Go on." Michael nudged her with his hip, trying to get her to go. The sound of guns cocking filled the air. Great, he hadn't even lowered his hands, and they were ready to take him out.

Carissa stood her ground and shook her head.

"Is there a problem, Pendarvis?"

Michael's teeth clench upon hearing his partner's voice. Of course Jareth would be here for this. They expected that, but the sound of his voice still raked against Michael's nerves.

"She won't come away from him," Demarco answered.

"Then get in there and get her out," Jareth ordered.

Demarco looked off to the right, where the team leader was poised, ready for action.

"Look." Michael lifted his hands up a little and watched the taut soldiers track his movements.

"There's no need for this; I'll come quietly." Relief passed a few of their eyes. They had all worked with Michael before and knew what he was capable of.

"Yeah right," Jareth called, "then release her from whatever spell you have on her, and let her go."

"Jareth," Michael said, shifting his head to better look at his partner, "you should know that I don't do magic."

"Then explain your hair."

Good point. Michael should have realized that could have caused some issues. Heavy magic use could leach the pigment out of a human. Of course they would think he had Carissa under some spell. There was no way they would believe it if he told them Carissa had turned him into a dragon.

"Go on," Michael urged her, but Carissa just stood her ground, glaring at Jareth. "I don't have a spell on her," he called to the men surrounding them. "She's just stubborn." That earned him a quick glare from Carissa.

In that moment of inattention, Demarco leaped at his chance and grabbed Carissa's hand to yank her out. Movement caught Carissa's eye, and she twisted away from Demarco, slamming into Michael as the loud pop of a gun went off. Pain ripped across Carissa's face as blood bloomed on her back, right above the part that covered Michael's heart.

The circle of Elites froze as Michael caught her. A roar rattled the park as magic rippled across Michael's skin.

Someone was going to pay dearly for hurting *Mine!.*

Chapter Nineteen

SCREAMS RANG OUT THROUGH THE PARK AS GUNFIRE barked from several of Eternity's Elites. The bullets bounced off the iridescent scales of the white dragon that had been one of their numbers. Michael crouched protectively over *Mine!*. These men had hurt her and were going to pay for it.

Letting out a great roar, Michael swung his tail, taking out three of the men behind him. He placed one clawed foot over *Mine!* so she was protected but wouldn't be crushed as he fought. Turning his attention to the man in front of him, Michael snapped him up and tossed him into one of the bushes. He really didn't want to hurt these men; they had been his friends. Well, he didn't want to hurt most of them. One was most definitely going to be hurting.

The sting of bullets on his left side had Michael turning to face his attacker. Balling up his claws, Michael swiped at the man, knocking him back. A few quick flaps of his great wings knocked the rest of the Elites off their feet. A few more shots hit Michael's back, but a swing of his tail took care of that attacker. They should know better than this. They were going to need something much bigger than the handguns they were trying to hit him with.

Looking around, Michael saw the one person he really wanted, hunkered down and taking aim. Michael roared in rage at his partner. He lunged at him, snapping his teeth but missing the man. He was just out of Michael's reach. He would have to relinquish his protective hold on *Mine!* to get to him. An answering roar came from the bushes where he had tossed Demarco. Michael snarled and pulled himself over *Mine!* as a green dragon shot into the air. Michael let go with another echoing roar, warning the new dragon off.

A bark of gunfire from Jareth brought Michael's attention back to the ground.

Demarco took the opportunity to dive-bomb Michael. Michael was nearly twice his size, but the unexpected impact sent Michael teetering forwards.

"*Mine!*" Michael roared as he stumbled forwards, trying not to crush Carissa. Dropping to his belly next to her, he tucked his wing around her. No matter what, he had to protect her. Michael turned his attention to her to make sure he hadn't injured her more. *Mine!* lay motionless under his wing. Rage turned his vision red, and he whipped his head back around to that son of a bitch who'd shot her.

Roaring, Michael dropped his wings loose so they scraped across the ground. *Mine!* would be safe under that shield. A great swing of his tail brought the fringy end around to smack Jareth off his feet. Lunging forwards, Michael snapped the fallen man up in his massive jaws.

Jareth screamed in terror as his gun jammed up.

"*Michael!*" Daniel's voice boomed across the chaos.

Michael whipped his head around to look as his boss, racing towards him. Kyle was only a step behind him. Michael closed his mouth and sucked on his partner, worrying him with his teeth. One good bite, and the man was toast. Smoke bubbled out of Michael's nostrils, startling him. Oh my, he could make flames! Maybe he should just roast him instead.

"*Don't do it!*" Daniel loped up to stand in front of Michael. "Killing him won't do you any good."

A growl rumbled up from Michael's chest. He lifted his wing, showing *Mine!*'s crumpled form, and then dropped it over her again, protectively.

The blood drained from Kyle's face, but he stayed where he was.

Smart man.

Demarco landed behind Daniel, watching Michael closely.

Michael's jaws clenched, making Jareth scream again.

"You will never clear your name if he's dead," Daniel yelled up at him.

The desire to crunch down on the man that hurt *Mine!* and the need to clear his name warred inside of him. His instincts demanded that he end what had hurt *Mine!*, but he couldn't be with *Mine!* if he killed the pathetic thing wiggling in his mouth.

Michael sucked on him, rolling him around in his mouth, considering his options. *Crunch or spit him out? Crunch or spit him out? Crunch or spit him out?* A tingle against his side drew his attention from the whimpering mouthful. *Mine!* sat up under his wing, rubbing his side. *Mine!* was alive! Her eyes held a note of begging that made his decision for him.

Opening his mouth, Michael dumped the sodden man out at Daniel's feet. He snorted before shifting back to his belly and curling his head up under his wing. *Mine!* leaned out and hugged his great nose.

She kissed it, borrowing the voice he wasn't using. "Thank you." Carissa rubbed her cheek between his nostrils. "Can you help me up?"

Michael let *Mine!* grab on to his scales as he

lifted her to her feet.

"Mine," she declared, and kissed him on the nose again.

Michael purred his contentment at being claimed. His head followed *Mine!* as she walked out from under his protective wing. The Elites he had knocked over were back up with guns trained on him, waiting for his next attack.

"Put those away!" Daniel called to the men surrounding Michael.

Michael's head shifted back and forth with a growled warning.

The men tensed up with guns aimed at him.

"They won't hurt her," Daniel reassured Michael. "*I said put them up!*" he bellowed to his squad.

Slowly, they lowered their guns, but no one actually holstered anything.

Daniel looked down at the mess Michael had made of Jareth. He was well slobbered and slightly chewed, but nothing a field kit couldn't fix. He squatted down so he could talk to him. "So, do you want to explain why you fired on an unarmed man giving himself up?"

Jareth looked up at his boss. "She wouldn't leave his side," he answered. "His hair was white. I thought he had her under a spell."

"It takes a better man than him to bespell me,"

Carissa growled at him. "No offense, love." She patted the side of Michael's head where it lay next to her.

He snorted his forgiveness.

Daniel looked over the woman, and then turned back to Jareth. "Of all the people here, you should know that Michael isn't a mage," he reprimanded him. "As you can see, he had another reason for the white hair." Daniel waved at the huge mound of white dragon sprawled in the grass. "But, you'd have known that if you had followed protocol and brought him in like you were ordered to." He looked around at the rest of the group still holding their positions. "Did I, or did I not, tell you to come out and collect him peacefully?"

The group was deathly still.

Daniel turned his attention back to Jareth. "I believe my exact words were, 'Michael is no longer a suspect in Carissa's abduction. He's waiting for you in the park. Please bring them both in, unharmed.'"

Disbelief and doubt swept across the faces of the Elites surrounding Michael.

"Isn't that what he told all of you?"

Heads shook around the group.

"No?" Daniel looked back down at Jareth.

"Sir?"

Daniel looked at the brave man. "Yes, McGee?"

"We were informed that Michael had been spotted in the park, and we were to bring him back by any means necessary."

"Any means necessary?" Daniel asked.

The solider nodded. "Any means necessary." In fact, most of the group nodded.

Daniel stood up, away from the worn man. "I think this might require a full inquiry—of this incident and everything in the last five years."

Jareth looked rather peaked and pale.

"McGee." Daniel looked over at the brave solider who had spoken up. "Why don't you, Charlie Mac, and Demarco head back to base and lock our friend here up. Oh, and while you're at it, there's a very interesting file on my desk that needs taken over to Internal Affairs. Give it to the investigator who's been working on Duncan's case. Apparently, someone's been leaving vital information out of his reports."

McGee's eye's narrowed as he caught the implication. They jumped to Michael's still form and then to Jareth before coming back to Daniel. "Yes, sir!" McGee and another heavier, dark-skinned man fished Jareth up from where he was sprawled. They patted him down, stripping him of his weapons, and frog-marched the man out of the park as Demarco's green-dragon form lumbered behind them.

Now that Jareth was dealt with, Daniel turned his attention to Carissa. "Are you hurt?"

She leaned against the boned frill at the back of Michael's head.

Michael's eye tracked Daniel's movements as he and Kyle approached her. A warning growl rumbled up from his chest.

The surrounding Elites raised their guns to point at the dragon.

"I said *put those away!*" Daniel's yell stopped the motion. "Meaning holster those pieces!"

Movement was reluctant, but the surrounding Eternity members tucked their guns away.

Carissa patted Michael soothingly. "I'm fine." She shifted so Daniel could see the bullet wound on her shoulder. The 9mm slug had just barely broken the skin. "I'm not stupid enough to come into a potential firefight without protection. I just hadn't expected it to hit that hard." Carissa moved her shoulder around, working the ache out of it. "Knocked the wind out of me for a few minutes. This big lug didn't even realize I'd cast protection spells on the both of us as we wandered the park."

Michael shifted so he could catch her in the corner of his eye. Protection spells? He vaguely remembered *Mine!*'s fingers tingling as she ran them over his butt. So she was spelling him, not caressing his ass. Michael snorted. He had liked it better when he thought the little gropes and tingles were because she liked his ass. Oh well, they had felt good.

"And you." Daniel finally turned his attention to the elephant in the room, or rather, the gigantic, white dragon drawing a crowd. "Damn, you're huge." He ran his eyes down Michael's side. "I think he might be bigger than you are." Daniel turned to look at Kyle.

"I think you're right." Kyle had been oddly silent through this entire exchange. His eyes kept drifting from Carissa to Michael and the protective way the large dragon guarded his sister.

"Well," Daniel sighed, "I'm sorry to say this, but I'm going to have to put you on administrative leave until further notice."

Michael nodded his understanding without disturbing *Mine!, who* was leaning into him. Man, she felt good there.

"Now, why don't you shift back so we can go sort this shit out."

"I don't think that's a good idea," Carissa interrupted before Michael could nod his head.

"Why not?"

"Decency laws," Carissa offered. "I don't think he stopped to take off his clothing before he shifted."

Michael snorted. Clothing had been the furthest thing from his mind at that moment. He vaguely remembered the sound of tearing. Laws were in place to allow dragons to shift, but a brash display of public nudity would still get you arrested.

"Point." Daniel gave him a considering look. "A blanket. We need a blanket."

Carissa let out a sigh of relief as she leaned against her bedroom door and engaged the lock. Alone at last! Well, not completely alone. Her eyes swept over Michael's broad back as he surveyed her quarters.

The last day had been grueling. After the chaos in the park, they had both been subject to medical care, followed by hours of interrogation at the hands of Eternity's Internal Affairs department. She had nearly taken someone's head off when they had tried to get her to part with Michael. He was hers, and no one was going to take him away from her—especially in a place where someone might hurt him. A few of his fellow Elites held tightly to their guns while Michael was around. As if they'd never seen a dragon before! But, that was over now.

Bless Daniel. He, of all those idiots her brother had arranged to protect dragons, had seen the connection between her and Michael. It was on his order that the Internal Affairs guys backed off and allowed her to stay with him, under the condition that she remain quiet. Which worked out fine, since she had to give Michael back his voice to answer their questions. She simply held his hand as they drilled him about his involvement with the missing dragons.

In good form, Michael sat contently, answering the same string of questions until the investigator was sure his story wouldn't change. Then, they had left them sitting in an overly bright interrogation room, but that hadn't bothered either of them much. Simply holding his hand, knowing that she had found the one man for her, made the entire event bearable.

Finally, Michael had been released into her custody by order of her brother. They had grabbed a couple of burgers before coming back here so Carissa could get changed. Her shirt currently had a bullet hole in it. Michael had insisted that she wear the leather jacket they had left in Daniel's office on their last visit. He had also tried to give her his shirt, but she put her foot down on that one.

Things with Eternity were starting to look better, but they had a lot to do before everything was settled. They still had to return Terrence's truck and pick up the motorcycle. Then, there was the issue of Michael's ruined home. But all of that could wait until later. Right now, Carissa had plans for Michael.

"There you are!" Michael snapped up his good leather jacket from where it hung over the arm of Carissa's couch. Tilly must have picked it up after she snuck them out. "I've missed you." He held it up, checking for damage. There were a few new scratches on it from Carissa's claws, but overall, it was fine.

Carissa smiled at his joy and stalked after him. What she had in mind didn't involve a leather coat.

"Here." Michael fished in one of the inside pockets and turned to find Carissa a lot closer then she had been. Surprise crossed his face as he held out a handful to her.

A seductive smile curled her lips as she took his offering: her jewels from the ball and a single, golden scale. Reaching up, she took the jacket from his hand and dropped it to the floor. A gentle hand on his chest pressed him backwards until his calves hit the couch and he went down to the cushions.

"Hello." Michael smiled as his hands came up to her hips.

Carissa slipped her knee up on one side of him and settled on his lap, facing him. Her fingers sorted through her things, pulling the scale out and letting the jewels spill to the floor behind her. Michael's hands slid lower, supporting her as she leaned forwards and ran the scale over his jaw line. She leaned in and placed a kiss on his lips, stealing his voice. "Mine," she purred as she pulled back before he could deepen the kiss.

A rumble of agreement issued from Michael's chest as he pulled her harder against him. Oh yes, he liked that idea.

Carissa saw a single objection pass through his ice-blue eyes, and he opened his mouth to voice it. "No." She shook her head, stopping him. "Like it or not, you are mine." She ran her fingers up through his hair, making his eyes close in sheer pleasure. "I claim you." This brought his eyes back open to look deeply into hers. "And tomorrow, I will give you this scale, so the whole world will see that you're mine." She ran the scale over his cheek again. "It will look beautiful set about right here." The hard edge scraped up over his temple and into his hairline.

He shivered at her touch. Well, this scale was probably too dead to do what she wanted with it, but he would have one of her scales. In addition to the desire darkening his eyes, there was shock and a single question. Did she know what sharing scales meant?

Carissa nearly laughed at him. Here she was, offering her life to him, and he was giving her a way out. A sign that he was truly her mate. The exchange of scales would bind them together irrevocably. It was painful and took a skilled mage, but once the scales were set, it marked them as a pair. Older pairs had entire sections of their hide that had taken on the color of their mate's scales. Michael would look good with a section of gold on his frill. If he were lucky, the color might even seep over into his human form as a lock of gold mixed into his silver hair. That would be perfect.

"Oh, yes." Carissa caressed him one more time. "I know what that means, and I will share a scale with you, if you'll have me."

Delight filled Michael's eyes, and his hands slid up her back pulling her in for a tight hug.

She laughed and wrapped her arms around his head as he nodded, rubbing his face into her chest. They would have to talk about a human marriage later, but that was a formality for others. The sharing of scales was the real bonding.

Leaning back, Carissa pressed her lips to his once again.

Michael growled in desire and deepened the kiss. His hands slipped back down to her hips, pulling her forwards until they were fitted together as tightly as their clothing would allow. Oh, yes. They had both been waiting for this since he had pinned her to the grass on Darien's lawn.

Heat bloomed in her as Michael pressed them together and worshipped at her lips. His tongue slipped into her mouth, promising all sorts of carnal delights. She shrugged off Michael's spare jacket as he rubbed against her rhythmically. Oh, their first time was definitely going to be hard and fast, followed by hours of slow exploration. She shivered with anticipation as his lips left hers and worked their way down to her throat. She nearly laughed at the sound of tearing as he shredded her shirt instead of relinquishing her long enough to take it off. Oh well, it was ruined anyway, but she decided she would gladly let him destroy any of her clothing as his mouth found her breasts.

A loud knock on the door broke into their moment.

"Carissa?" Tilly's voice called through the door. The handle wiggled as her best friend tried to let herself in.

Carissa thanked God that she had locked it on her way in.

"I know you're in there." The knock sounded again.

Michael closed his teeth on her nipple and growled his frustration at the interruption. He rubbed his swollen length against her core.

Carissa let out a sigh. Tilly had the worst timing. Should she stop this and let her best friend in?

Michael's hands slipped around, loosening the zipper on her jeans before slipping down the back of her pants and caressing her ass. He rubbed her against him again as his mouth moved to feast on the other breast.

The knock sounded on the door again as Tilly called to them.

No, Tilly could wait. Carissa was not going to let anything else interrupt them again. She was going to have him. *Now.* The world could wait—for days if need be. And once she'd had her fill, once they had explored each other thoroughly in human form, she would convince him to shift to dragon for a whole new realm of pleasures. And then, only then, would she let the world back in.

Acknowledgements

WELCOME ALL OF YOU THAT HAVE MADE IT TO THE END of the book. I truly hope you enjoyed it as much as I enjoyed writing. This story started out as something else to keep my sister entertained during her deployment. It hadn't occurred to me that anyone else would be interested in it until Marya asked for dragon book. As a fellow lover of dragons, she wanted the opportunity to do a cover with dragons on it. I wasn't sure if the ladies at CTP would like it—it was different than my other books, but I sent it in hoping it would make the cut. I'm so glad I did.

A lot of people went into making this possible. I would like to thank my friends and family for supporting me as I toiled away at all hours to finish the original manuscript, Marya for making the request for the book, Sherry for loving it enough to let it into the girls, and everyone that put hours into getting it ready to be published. You are all loved. Thank you.

ORIGINALLY FROM OHIO, JULIE ALWAYS DREAMED OF A job in science. Either shooting for the stars or delving into the mysteries of volcanoes. But, life never leads where you expect. In 2007, she moved to Mississippi to be with her significant other.

Now a mother of a hyperactive red headed boy, what time she's not chasing down dirty socks and unsticking toys from the ceiling is spent crafting worlds readers can get lost it. Julie is a self-proclaimed bibliophile and lover of big words. She likes hiking, frogs, interesting earrings, and a plethora of other fun things.